**Replacement costs will be
billed after 42 days overdue.**

FRANKLIN PARK PUBLIC LIBRARY
FRANKLIN PARK, ILL.

Each borrower is held responsible for all library material drawn on his card and for fines accruing on the same. No material will be issued until such fine has been paid.

All injuries to library material beyond reasonable wear and all losses shall be made good to the satisfaction of the Librarian.

Jimmy Gownley's AMELIA RULES!™

The Gym Class System

Atheneum Books for Young Readers
New York London Toronto Sydney

Spotlight

VISIT US AT
www.abdopublishing.com

Reinforced library bound edition published in 2011 by Spotlight, a division of the ABDO Group, 8000 West 78th Street, Edina, Minnesota 55439. Spotlight produces high-quality reinforced library bound editions for schools and libraries. Published by agreement with Atheneum Books for Young Readers, an imprint of Simon & Schuster Children's Publishing Division.

Antheneum Books for Young Readers
An imprint of Simon & Schuster Children's Publishing Division
1230 Avenue of the Americans, New York, NY 10020

Printed in the United States of America, Melrose Park, Illinois.
052010
092010
 This book contains at least 10% recycled materials.

Library of Congress Cataloging-in-Publication Data

Gownley, Jimmy.
  Amelia and the gym class system / Jimmy Gownley. -- Reinforced library bound ed.
    p. cm. -- (Jimmy Gownley's Amelia rules! ; #2)
  Summary: Amelia recalls her first days at Joe McCarthy Elementary, where she attends fourth grade.
  ISBN 978-1-59961-788-6
  1. Graphic novels. [1. Graphic novels. 2. Schools--Fiction.] I. Title.
  PZ7.7.G69Ai 2010
  741.5'973--dc22   2010006193

All Spotlight books have reinforced library bindings and
are manufactured in the United States of America.

With Love and Thanks
to Mom and Dad...

With appreciation for
the Vision and Faith of
Joe, John, Jerry, and Bill...

And with gratitude for
the Patience and Friendship
of Michael...

This book is dedicated with love...
for Karen.

J-GN
AMELIA RULES
399-7221

The Gym
Class System

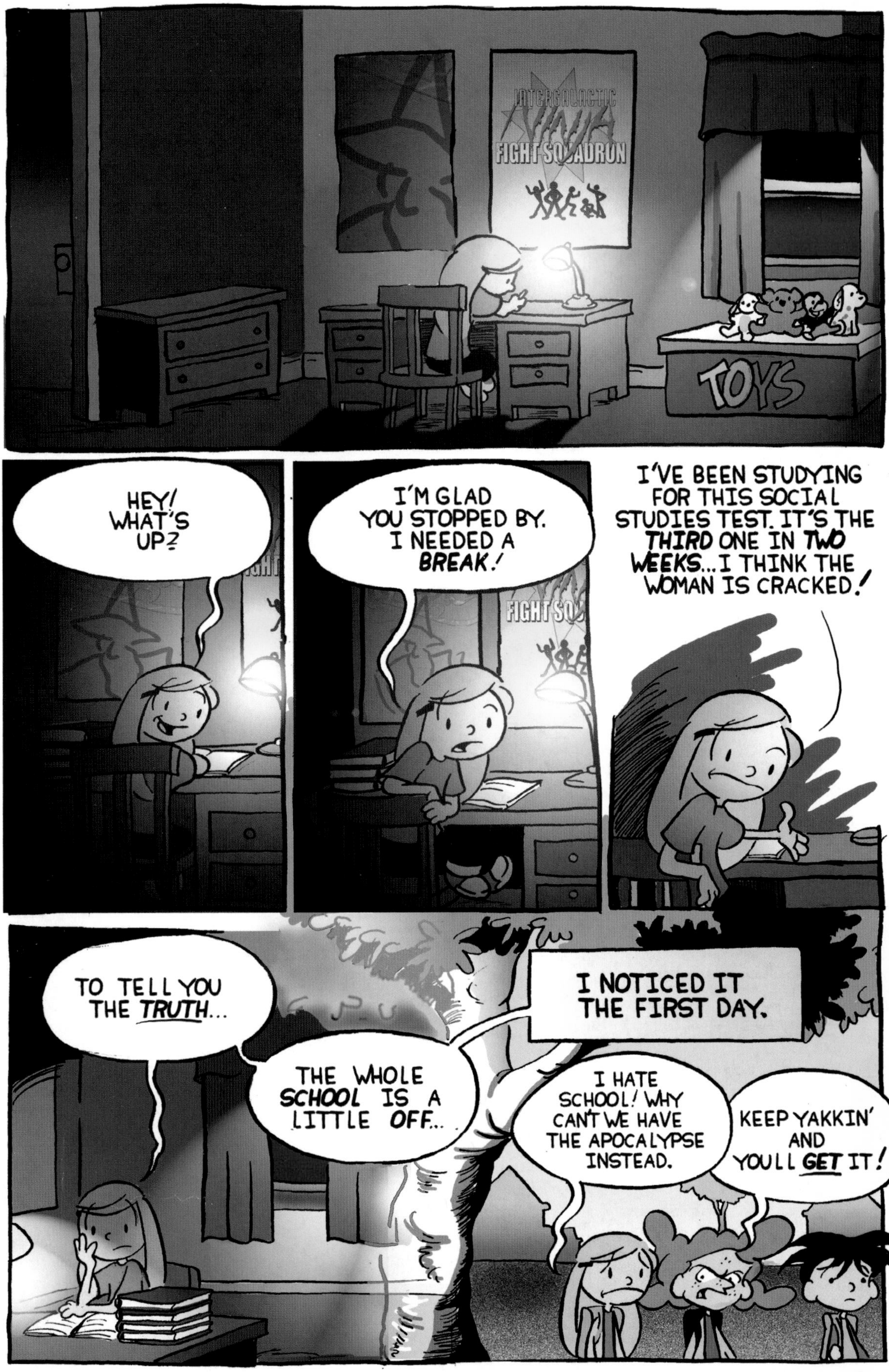
INTERGALACTIC NINJA FIGHT SQUADRON
TOYS
HEY! WHAT'S UP?
I'M GLAD YOU STOPPED BY. I NEEDED A BREAK!
I'VE BEEN STUDYING FOR THIS SOCIAL STUDIES TEST. IT'S THE THIRD ONE IN TWO WEEKS... I THINK THE WOMAN IS CRACKED!
TO TELL YOU THE TRUTH...
THE WHOLE SCHOOL IS A LITTLE OFF...
I NOTICED IT THE FIRST DAY.
I HATE SCHOOL! WHY CAN'T WE HAVE THE APOCALYPSE INSTEAD.
KEEP YAKKIN' AND YOU'LL GET IT!

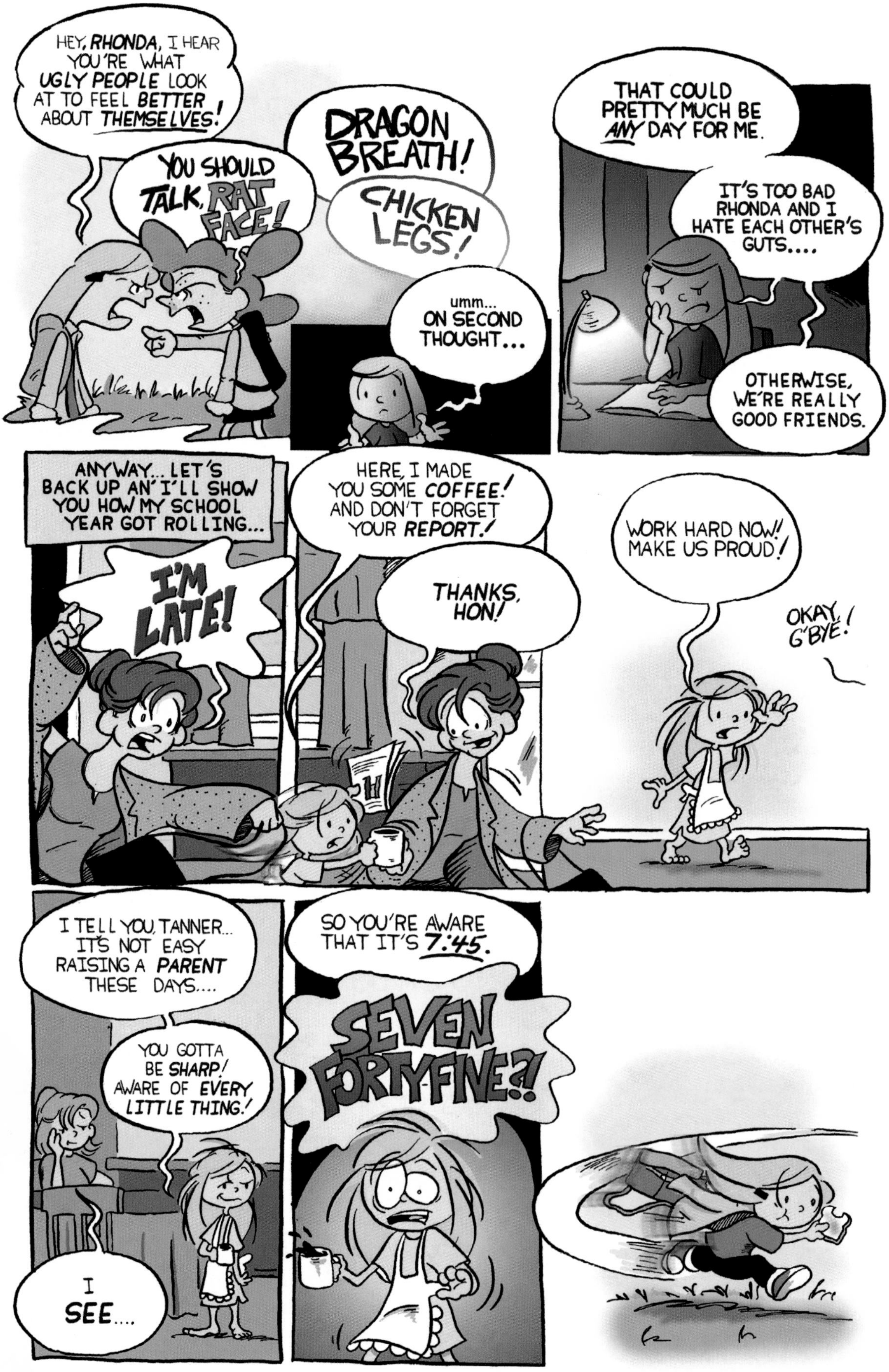
HEY, RHONDA, I HEAR YOU'RE WHAT UGLY PEOPLE LOOK AT TO FEEL BETTER ABOUT THEMSELVES!
YOU SHOULD TALK, RAT FACE!
DRAGON BREATH!
CHICKEN LEGS!
umm... ON SECOND THOUGHT...
THAT COULD PRETTY MUCH BE ANY DAY FOR ME.
IT'S TOO BAD RHONDA AND I HATE EACH OTHER'S GUTS....
OTHERWISE, WE'RE REALLY GOOD FRIENDS.
ANYWAY... LET'S BACK UP AN' I'LL SHOW YOU HOW MY SCHOOL YEAR GOT ROLLING...
I'M LATE!
HERE, I MADE YOU SOME COFFEE! AND DON'T FORGET YOUR REPORT!
THANKS, HON!
WORK HARD NOW! MAKE US PROUD!
OKAY, G'BYE!
I TELL YOU, TANNER... IT'S NOT EASY RAISING A PARENT THESE DAYS....
YOU GOTTA BE SHARP! AWARE OF EVERY LITTLE THING!
I SEE....
SO YOU'RE AWARE THAT IT'S 7:45.
SEVEN FORTYFIVE?!

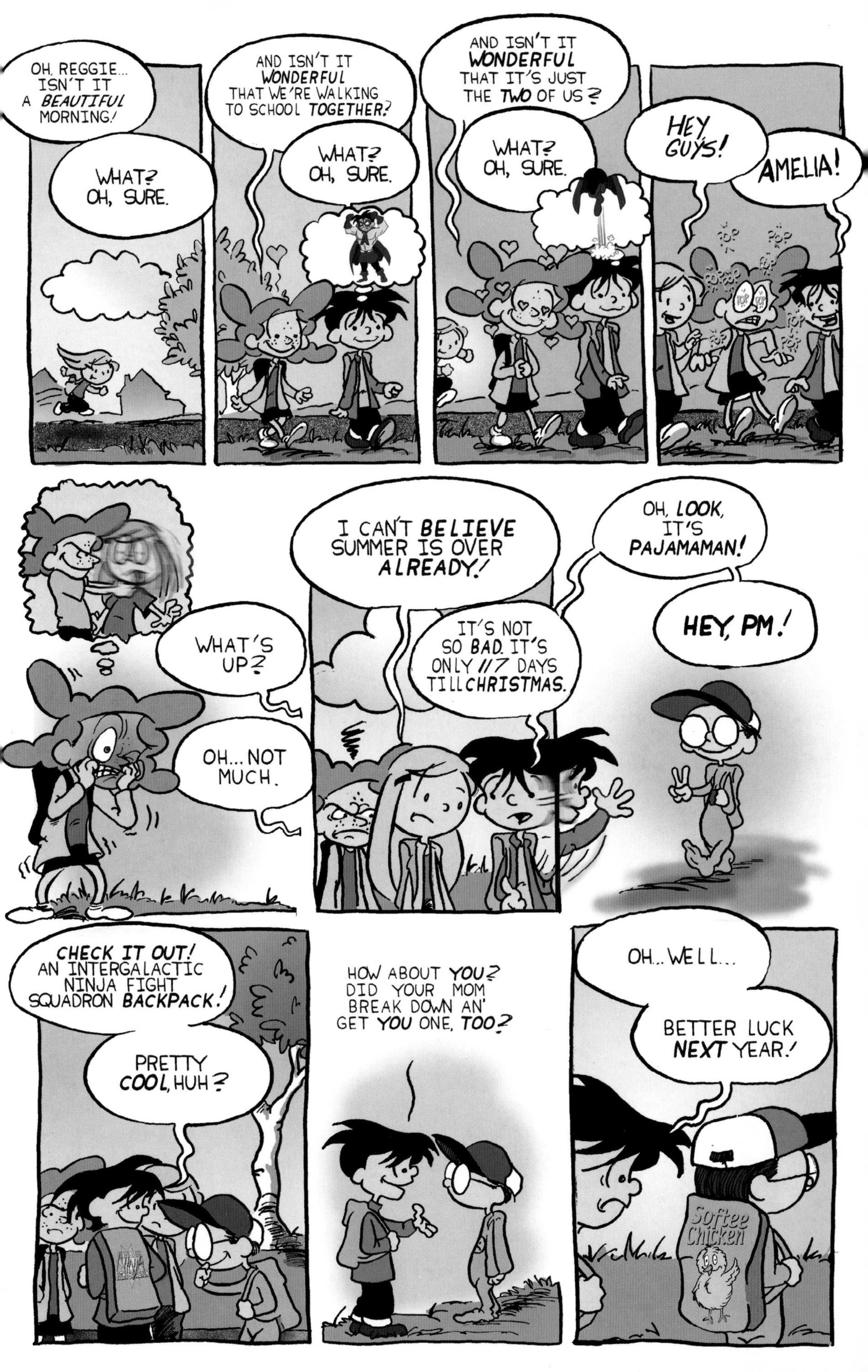
OH, REGGIE... ISN'T IT A BEAUTIFUL MORNING!
WHAT? OH, SURE.
AND ISN'T IT WONDERFUL THAT WE'RE WALKING TO SCHOOL TOGETHER?
WHAT? OH, SURE.
AND ISN'T IT WONDERFUL THAT IT'S JUST THE TWO OF US?
WHAT? OH, SURE.
HEY GUYS!
AMELIA!
POP
WHAT'S UP?
OH... NOT MUCH.
I CAN'T BELIEVE SUMMER IS OVER ALREADY!
IT'S NOT SO BAD. IT'S ONLY 117 DAYS TILL CHRISTMAS.
OH, LOOK, IT'S PAJAMAMAN!
HEY, PM!
CHECK IT OUT! AN INTERGALACTIC NINJA FIGHT SQUADRON BACKPACK!
PRETTY COOL, HUH?
HOW ABOUT YOU? DID YOUR MOM BREAK DOWN AN' GET YOU ONE, TOO?
OH... WELL...
BETTER LUCK NEXT YEAR!
Softee Chicken

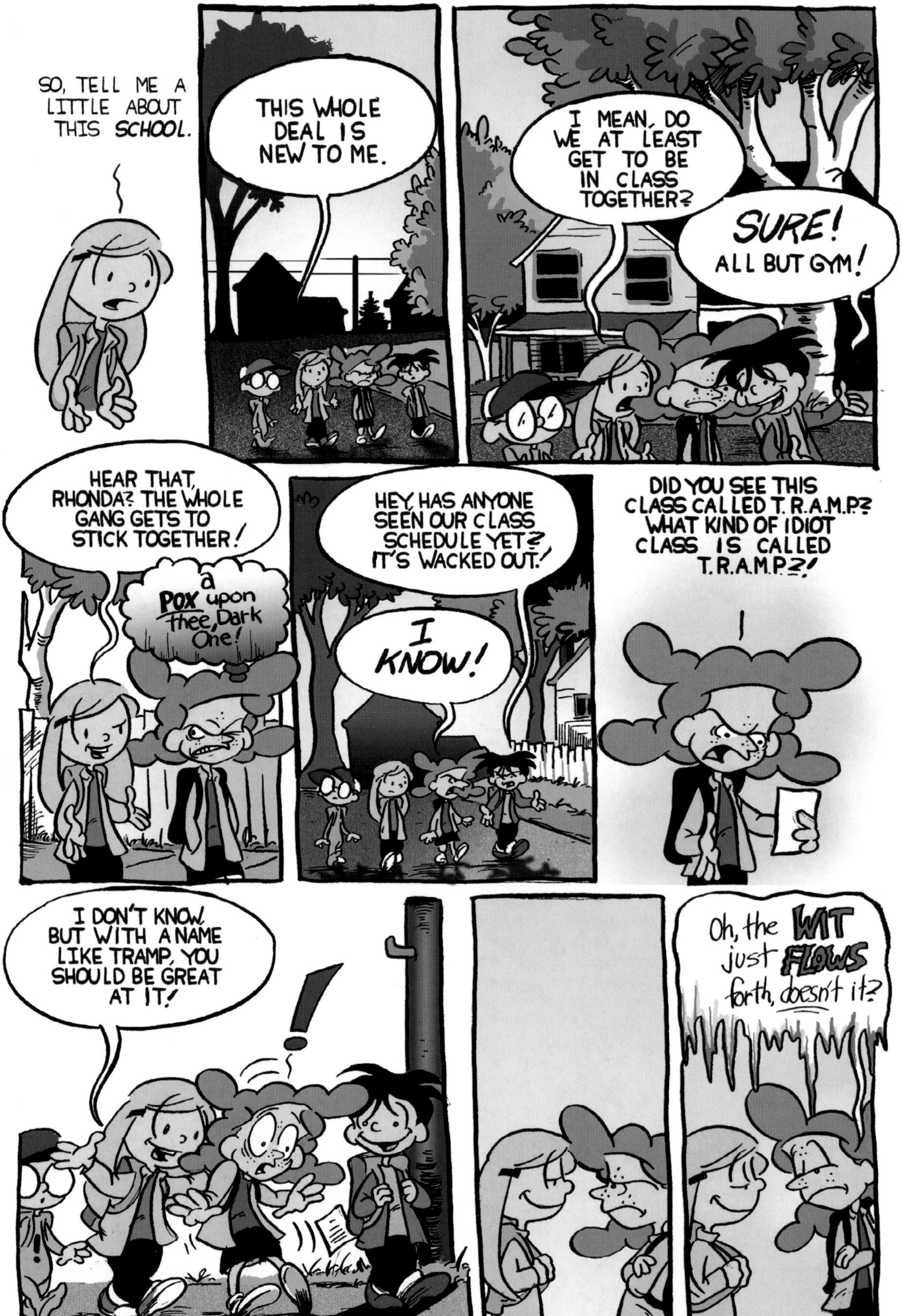
SO, TELL ME A LITTLE ABOUT THIS SCHOOL.
THIS WHOLE DEAL IS NEW TO ME.
I MEAN, DO WE AT LEAST GET TO BE IN CLASS TOGETHER?
SURE! ALL BUT GYM!
HEAR THAT, RHONDA? THE WHOLE GANG GETS TO STICK TOGETHER!
a POX upon thee, Dark One!
HEY, HAS ANYONE SEEN OUR CLASS SCHEDULE YET? IT'S WACKED OUT!
I KNOW!
DID YOU SEE THIS CLASS CALLED T.R.A.M.P.? WHAT KIND OF IDIOT CLASS IS CALLED T.R.A.M.P.?!
I DON'T KNOW. BUT WITH A NAME LIKE TRAMP, YOU SHOULD BE GREAT AT IT!
!
Oh, the WIT just FLOWS forth, doesn't it?

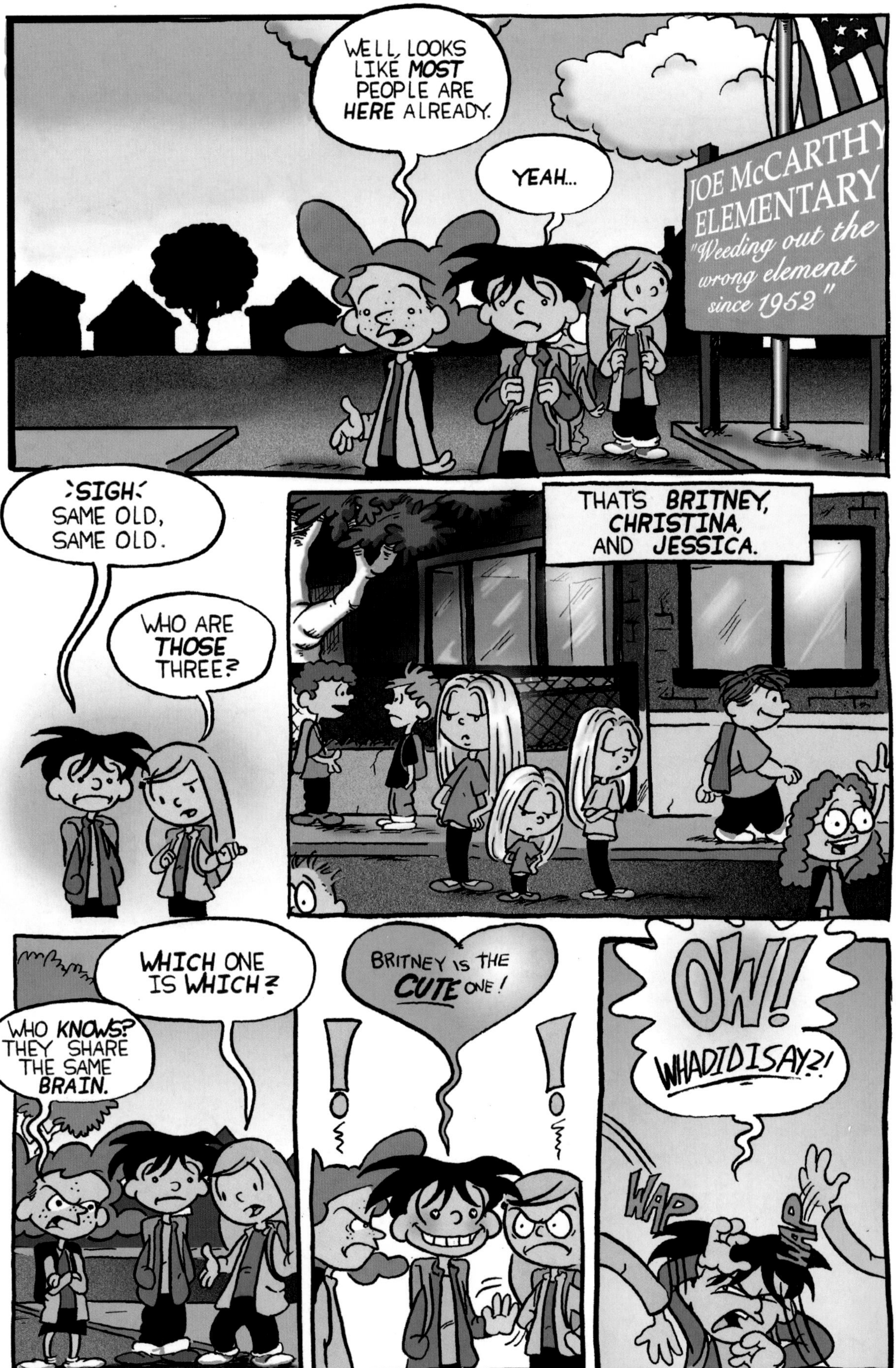
WELL, LOOKS LIKE MOST PEOPLE ARE HERE ALREADY.
YEAH...
JOE McCARTHY ELEMENTARY "Weeding out the wrong element since 1952"
SIGH SAME OLD, SAME OLD.
WHO ARE THOSE THREE?
THAT'S BRITNEY, CHRISTINA, AND JESSICA.
WHICH ONE IS WHICH?
WHO KNOWS? THEY SHARE THE SAME BRAIN.
BRITNEY IS THE CUTE ONE!
!
!
OW!
WHADIDISAY?!
WAP
WAP

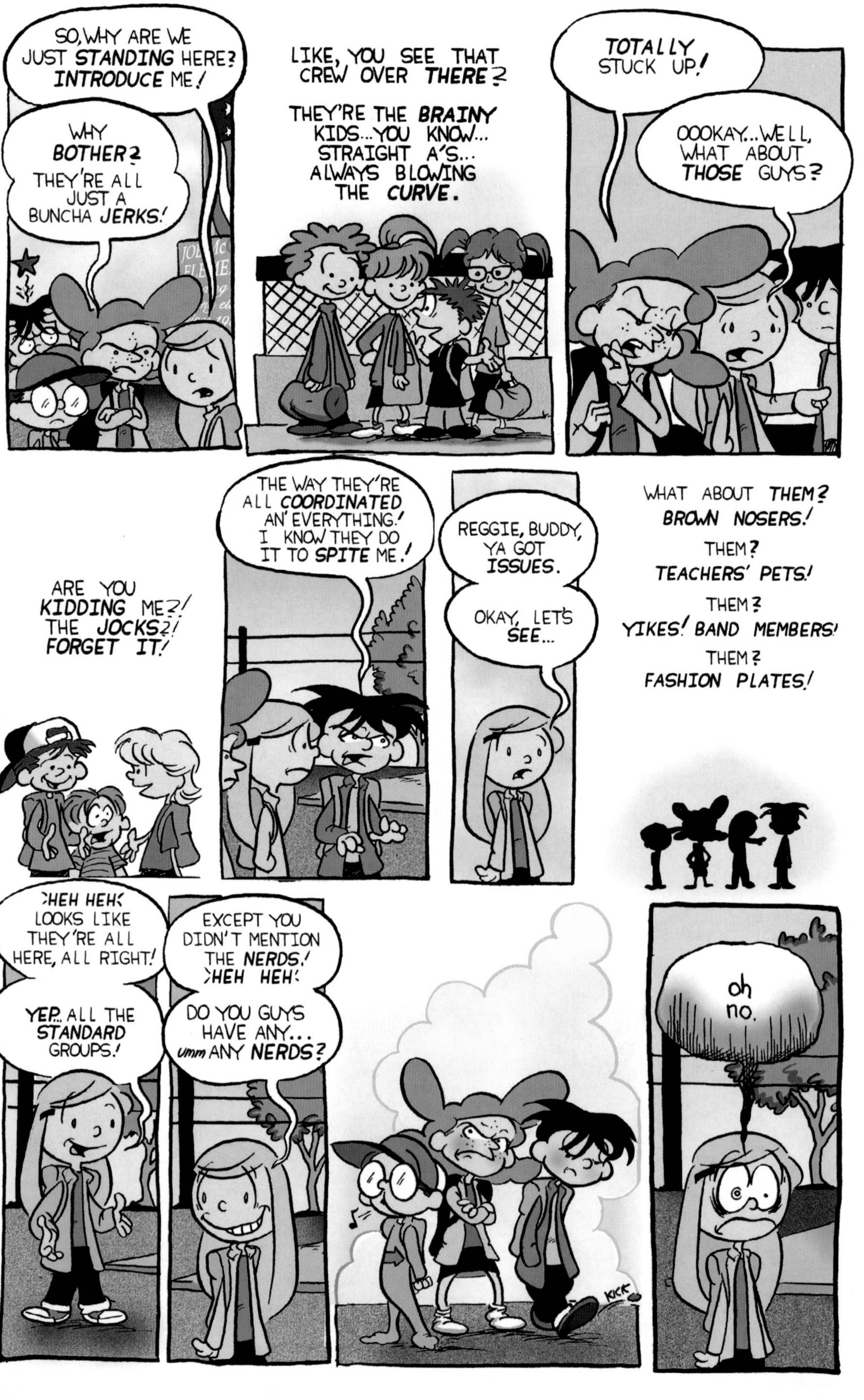
SO, WHY ARE WE JUST STANDING HERE? INTRODUCE ME!
WHY BOTHER? THEY'RE ALL JUST A BUNCHA JERKS!
LIKE, YOU SEE THAT CREW OVER THERE?
THEY'RE THE BRAINY KIDS... YOU KNOW... STRAIGHT A'S... ALWAYS BLOWING THE CURVE.
TOTALLY STUCK UP!
OOOKAY... WELL, WHAT ABOUT THOSE GUYS?
ARE YOU KIDDING ME?! THE JOCKS?! FORGET IT!
THE WAY THEY'RE ALL COORDINATED AN' EVERYTHING! I KNOW THEY DO IT TO SPITE ME!
REGGIE, BUDDY, YA GOT ISSUES.
OKAY, LET'S SEE...
WHAT ABOUT THEM? BROWN NOSERS!
THEM? TEACHERS' PETS!
THEM? YIKES! BAND MEMBERS!
THEM? FASHION PLATES!
>HEH HEH< LOOKS LIKE THEY'RE ALL HERE, ALL RIGHT!
YEP... ALL THE STANDARD GROUPS!
EXCEPT YOU DIDN'T MENTION THE NERDS! >HEH HEH<
DO YOU GUYS HAVE ANY... umm ANY NERDS?
KICK
oh no.

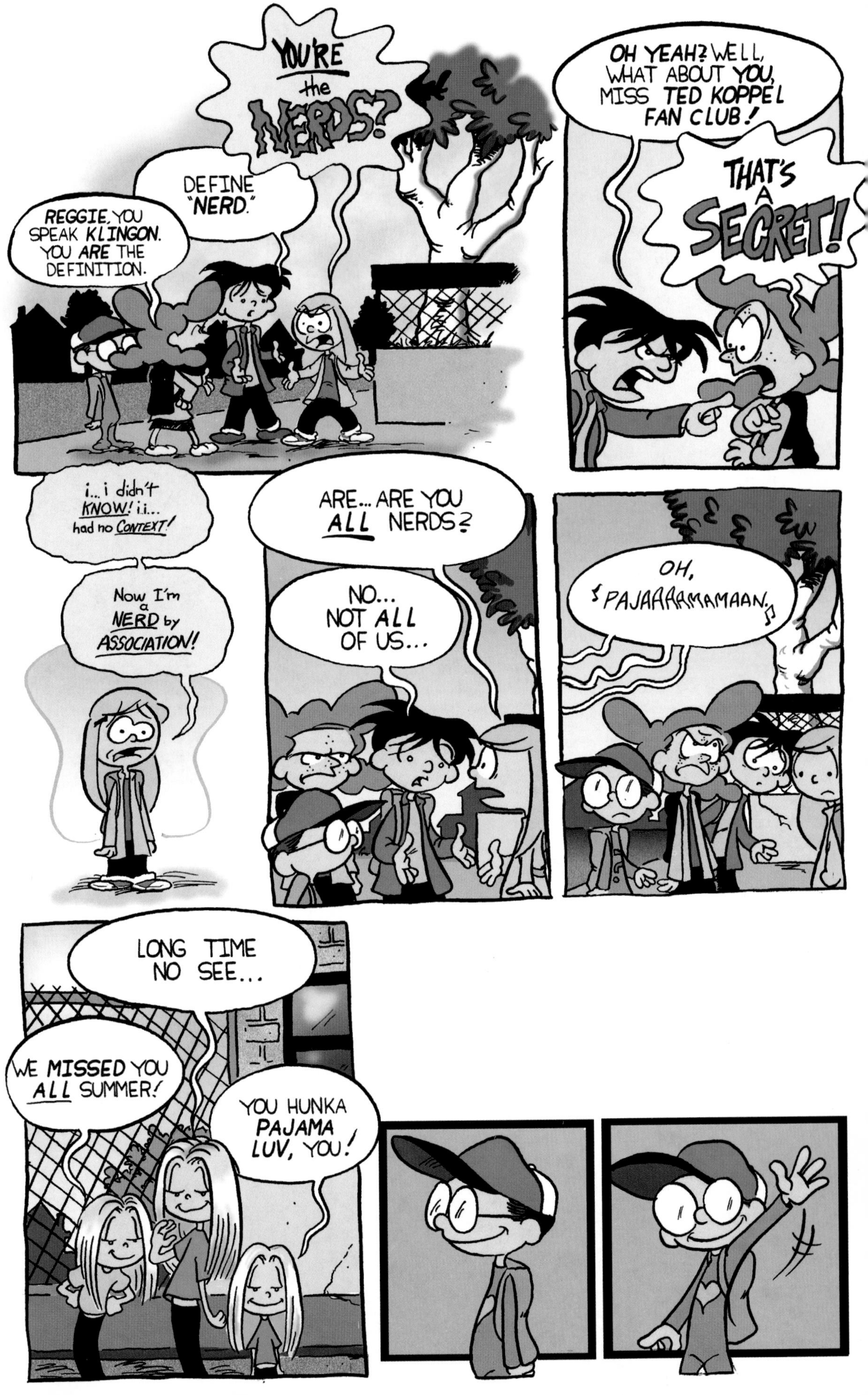

YOU'RE the NERDS?
DEFINE "NERD."
REGGIE, YOU SPEAK KLINGON. YOU ARE THE DEFINITION.
OH YEAH? WELL, WHAT ABOUT YOU, MISS TED KOPPEL FAN CLUB!
THAT'S A SECRET!
i... i didn't KNOW! i.i... had no CONTEXT!
Now I'm a NERD by ASSOCIATION!
ARE... ARE YOU ALL NERDS?
NO... NOT ALL OF US...
OH, PAJAAAAMAMAAN.
LONG TIME NO SEE...
WE MISSED YOU ALL SUMMER!
YOU HUNKA PAJAMA LUV, YOU!

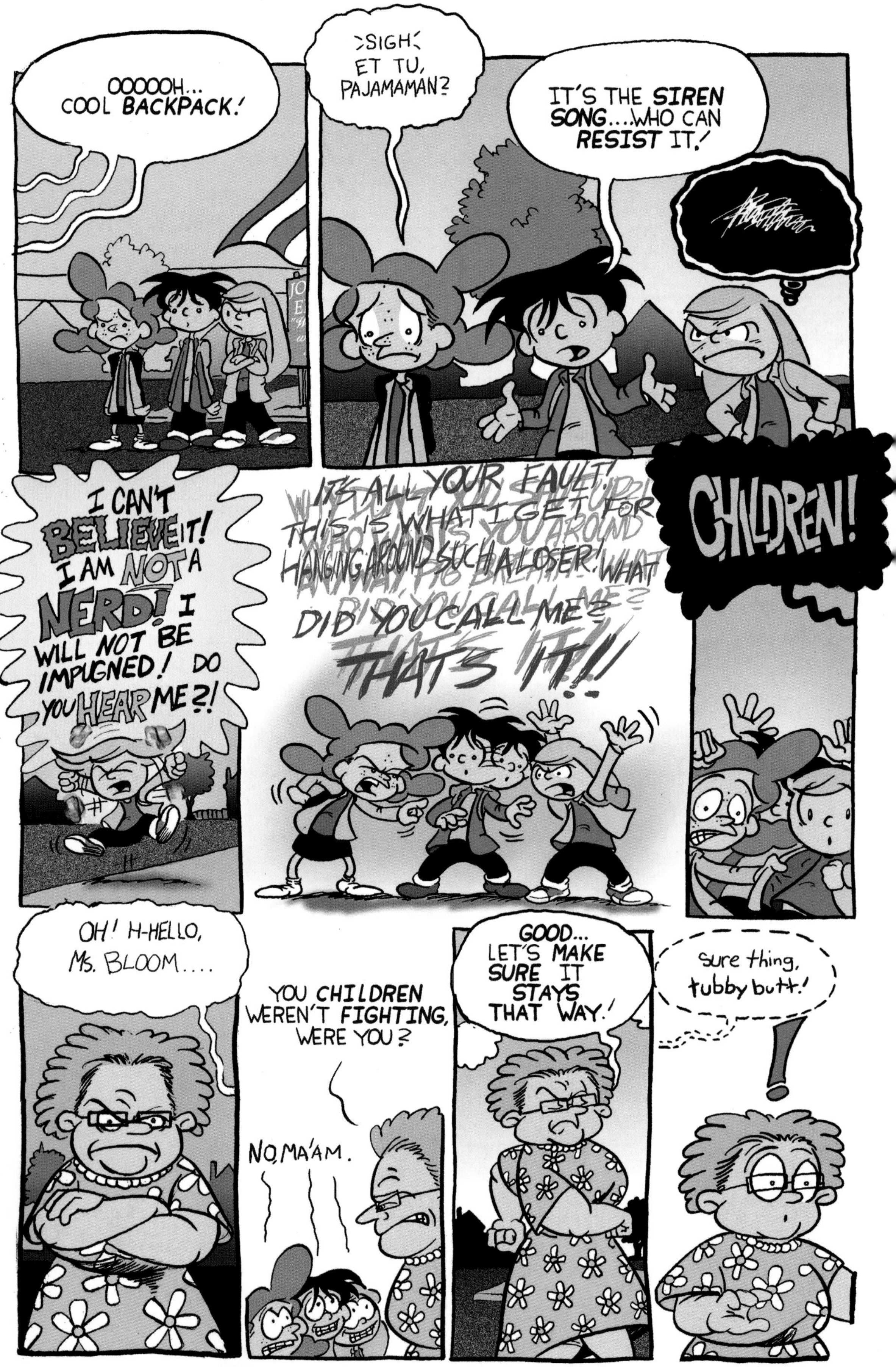

OOOOOH... COOL BACKPACK!
>SIGH< ET TU, PAJAMAMAN?
IT'S THE SIREN SONG...WHO CAN RESIST IT!
I CAN'T BELIEVE IT! I AM NOT A NERD! I WILL NOT BE IMPUGNED! DO YOU HEAR ME?!
IT'S ALL YOUR FAULT! THIS IS WHAT I GET FOR HANGING AROUND SUCH A LOSER! WHAT DID YOU CALL ME? THAT'S IT!!
CHILDREN!
OH! H-HELLO, MS. BLOOM....
YOU CHILDREN WEREN'T FIGHTING, WERE YOU?
NO, MA'AM.
GOOD... LET'S MAKE SURE IT STAYS THAT WAY!
Sure thing, tubby butt!
!

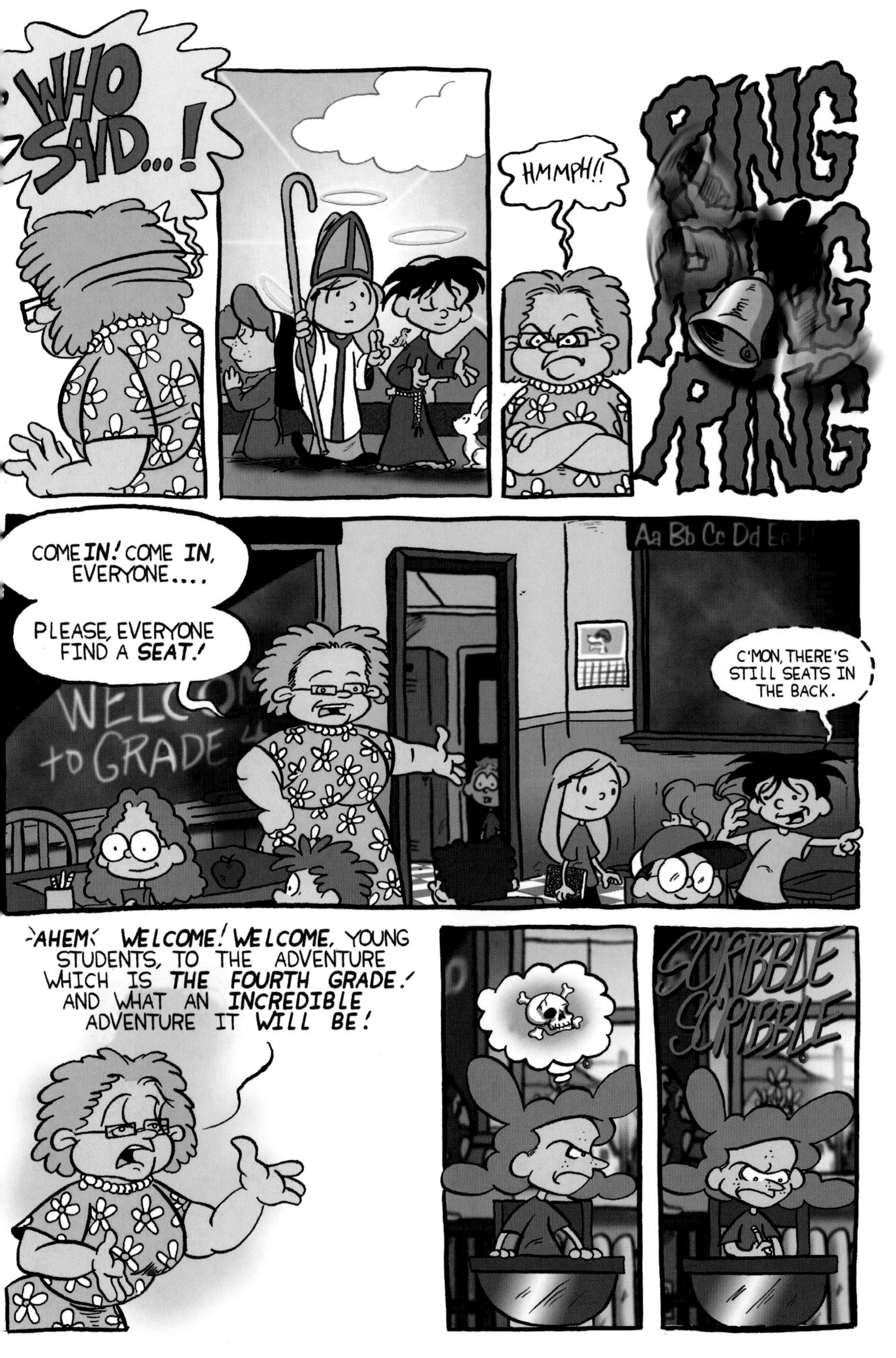
WHO SAID...!
HMMPH!!
RING RING RING
COME IN! COME IN, EVERYONE....
PLEASE, EVERYONE FIND A SEAT!
Aa Bb Cc Dd Ee
WELCO
to GRADE
C'MON, THERE'S STILL SEATS IN THE BACK.
-AHEM- WELCOME! WELCOME, YOUNG STUDENTS, TO THE ADVENTURE WHICH IS THE FOURTH GRADE! AND WHAT AN INCREDIBLE ADVENTURE IT WILL BE!
SCRIBBLE SCRIBBLE

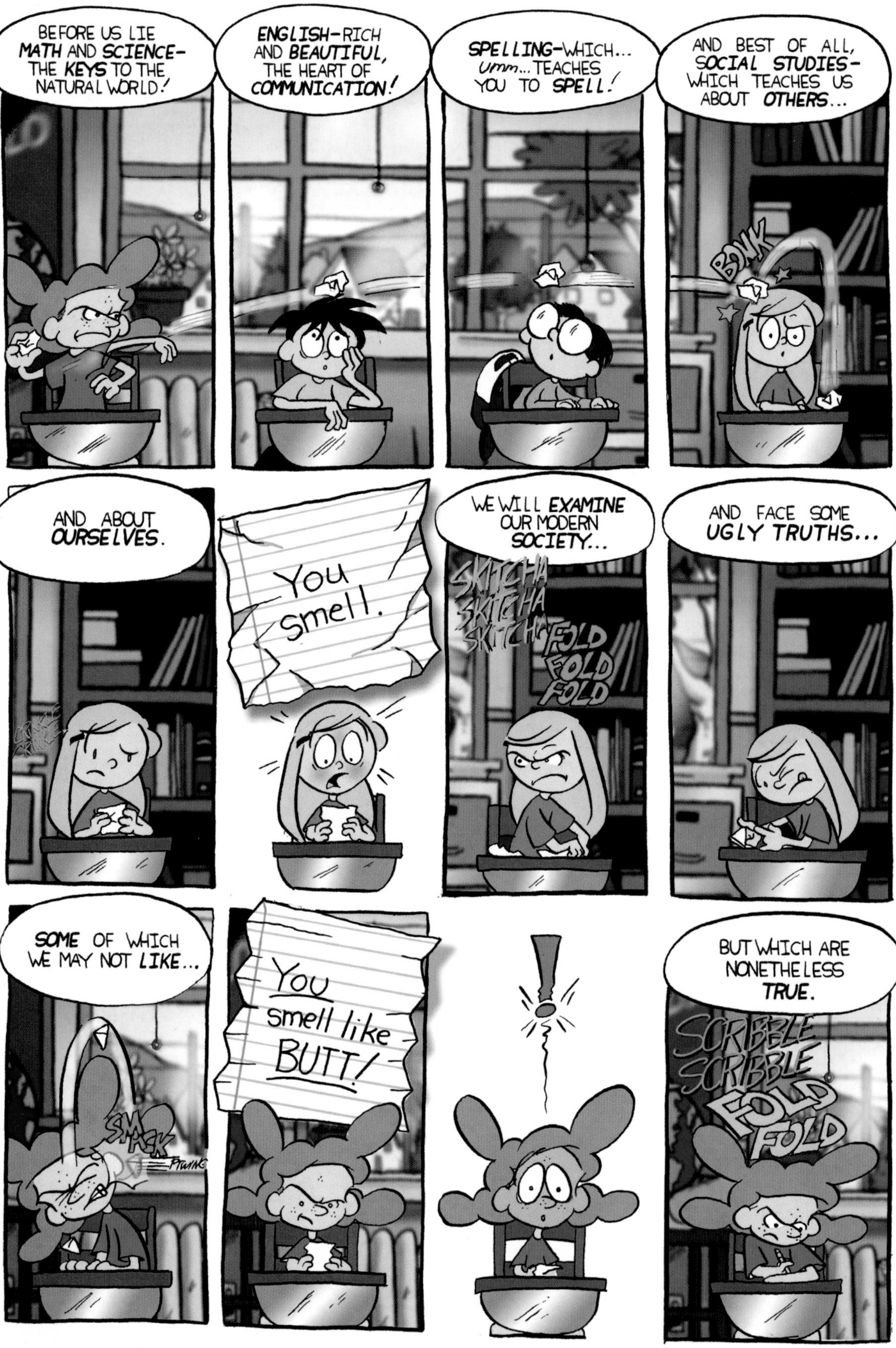
BEFORE US LIE MATH AND SCIENCE- THE KEYS TO THE NATURAL WORLD!
ENGLISH-RICH AND BEAUTIFUL, THE HEART OF COMMUNICATION!
SPELLING-WHICH... UMM... TEACHES YOU TO SPELL!
AND BEST OF ALL, SOCIAL STUDIES- WHICH TEACHES US ABOUT OTHERS...
BONK
AND ABOUT OURSELVES.
You smell.
WE WILL EXAMINE OUR MODERN SOCIETY...
SKITCHA SKITCHA SKITCHA
FOLD FOLD FOLD
AND FACE SOME UGLY TRUTHS...
SOME OF WHICH WE MAY NOT LIKE...
SMACK
PTWING
You smell like BUTT!
!
BUT WHICH ARE NONETHELESS TRUE.
SCRIBBLE SCRIBBLE
FOLD FOLD

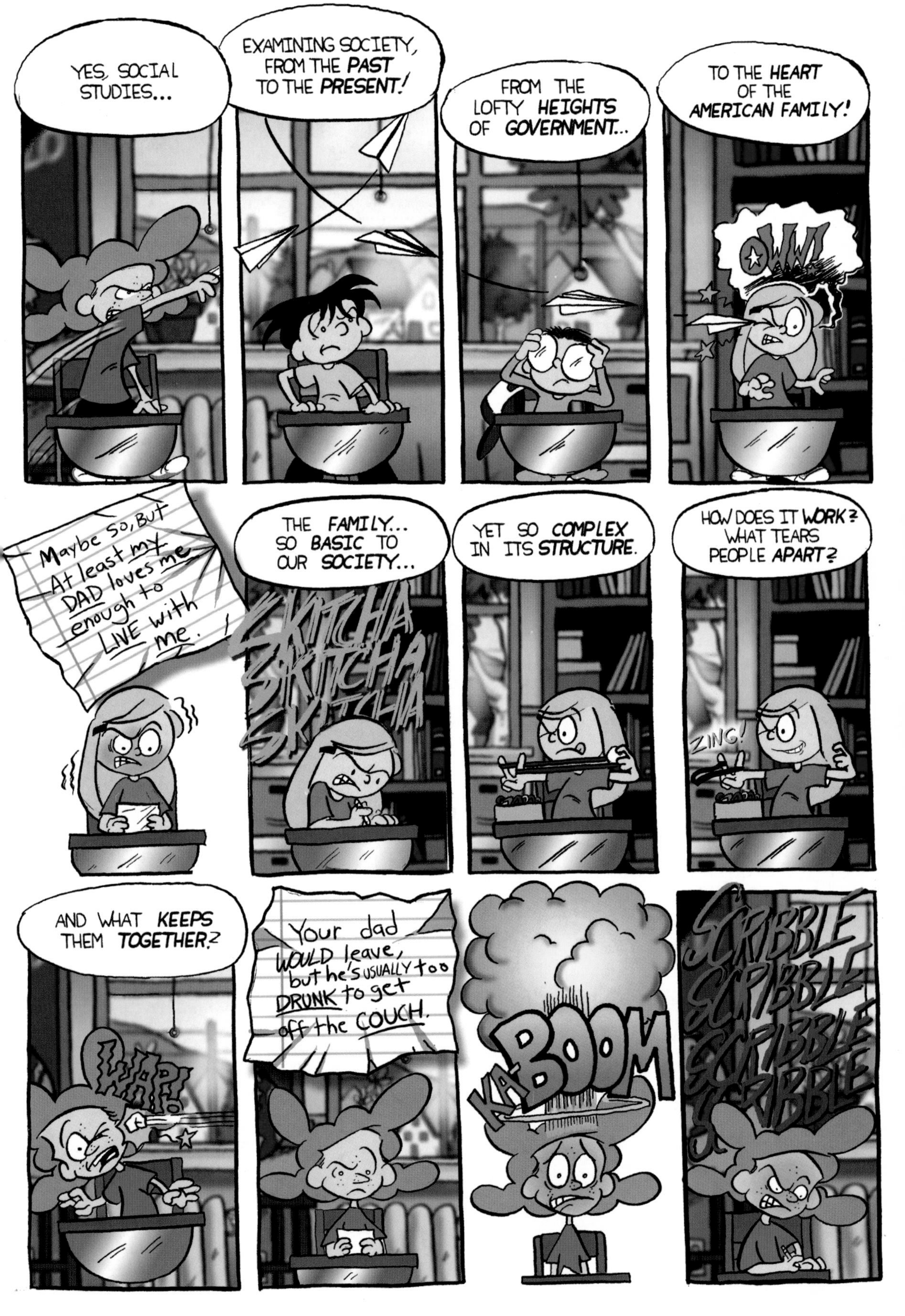
YES, SOCIAL STUDIES...
EXAMINING SOCIETY, FROM THE PAST TO THE PRESENT!
FROM THE LOFTY HEIGHTS OF GOVERNMENT...
TO THE HEART OF THE AMERICAN FAMILY!
OWW!
Maybe so, But At least my DAD loves me enough to LIVE with me.
THE FAMILY... SO BASIC TO OUR SOCIETY...
SKITCHA SKITCHA SKITCHA
YET SO COMPLEX IN ITS STRUCTURE.
HOW DOES IT WORK? WHAT TEARS PEOPLE APART?
ZING!
AND WHAT KEEPS THEM TOGETHER?
WAP!
Your dad WOULD leave, but he's USUALLY too DRUNK to get off the COUCH.
KA-BOOM
SCRIBBLE SCRIBBLE SCRIBBLE SCRIBBLE

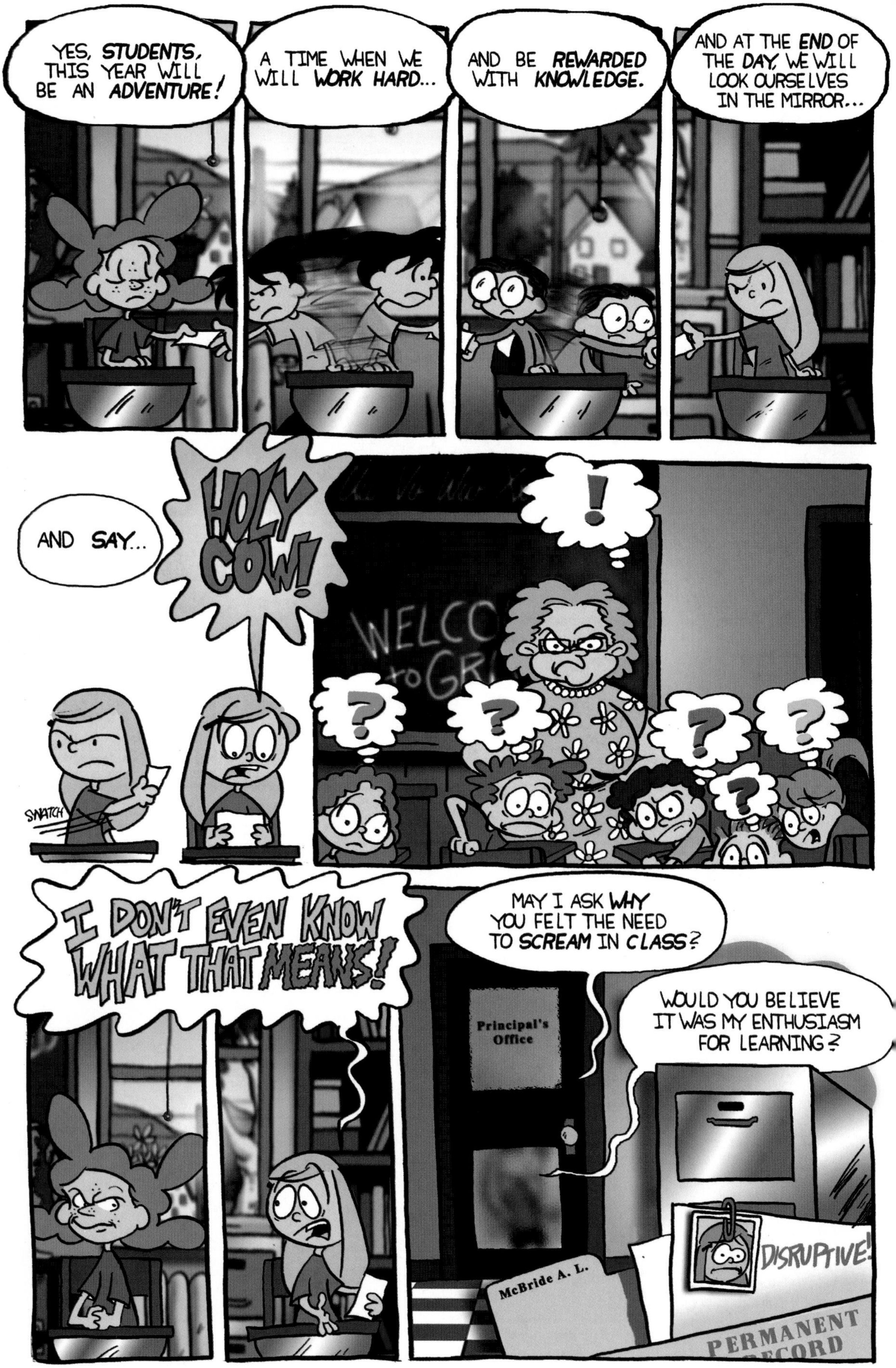
YES, STUDENTS, THIS YEAR WILL BE AN ADVENTURE!
A TIME WHEN WE WILL WORK HARD...
AND BE REWARDED WITH KNOWLEDGE.
AND AT THE END OF THE DAY, WE WILL LOOK OURSELVES IN THE MIRROR...
AND SAY...
HOLY COW!
!
SNATCH
WELCO to GR
?
?
?
?
?
I DON'T EVEN KNOW WHAT THAT MEANS!
MAY I ASK WHY YOU FELT THE NEED TO SCREAM IN CLASS?
Principal's Office
WOULD YOU BELIEVE IT WAS MY ENTHUSIASM FOR LEARNING?
McBride A. L.
DISRUPTIVE!
PERMANENT RECORD

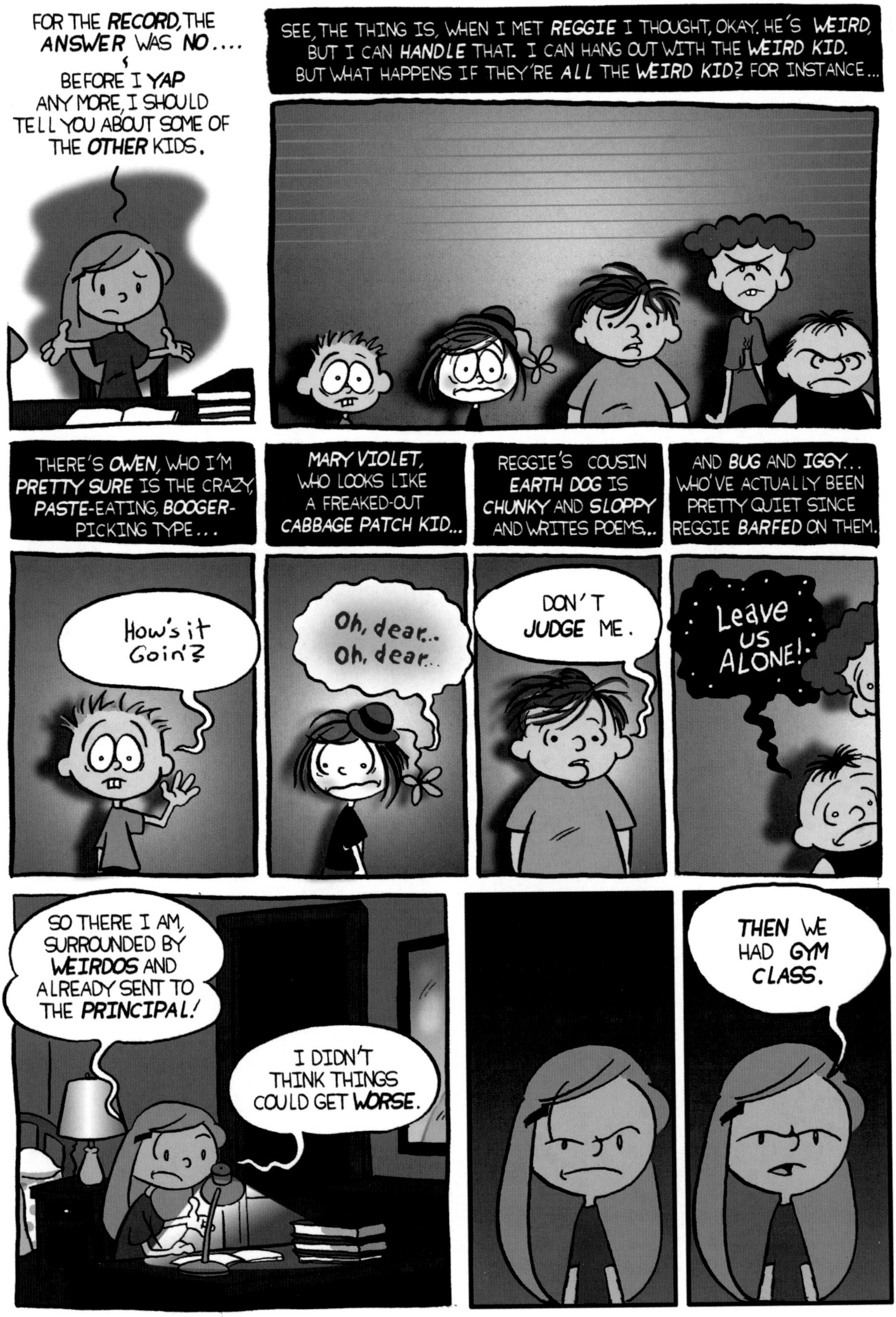
FOR THE RECORD, THE ANSWER WAS NO.... & BEFORE I YAP ANY MORE, I SHOULD TELL YOU ABOUT SOME OF THE OTHER KIDS.
SEE, THE THING IS, WHEN I MET REGGIE I THOUGHT, OKAY. HE'S WEIRD, BUT I CAN HANDLE THAT. I CAN HANG OUT WITH THE WEIRD KID. BUT WHAT HAPPENS IF THEY'RE ALL THE WEIRD KID? FOR INSTANCE...
THERE'S OWEN, WHO I'M PRETTY SURE IS THE CRAZY, PASTE-EATING, BOOGER-PICKING TYPE...
How's it Goin'?
MARY VIOLET, WHO LOOKS LIKE A FREAKED-OUT CABBAGE PATCH KID...
Oh, dear... Oh, dear...
REGGIE'S COUSIN EARTH DOG IS CHUNKY AND SLOPPY AND WRITES POEMS...
DON'T JUDGE ME.
AND BUG AND IGGY... WHO'VE ACTUALLY BEEN PRETTY QUIET SINCE REGGIE BARFED ON THEM.
Leave us ALONE!
SO THERE I AM, SURROUNDED BY WEIRDOS AND ALREADY SENT TO THE PRINCIPAL!
I DIDN'T THINK THINGS COULD GET WORSE.
THEN WE HAD GYM CLASS.

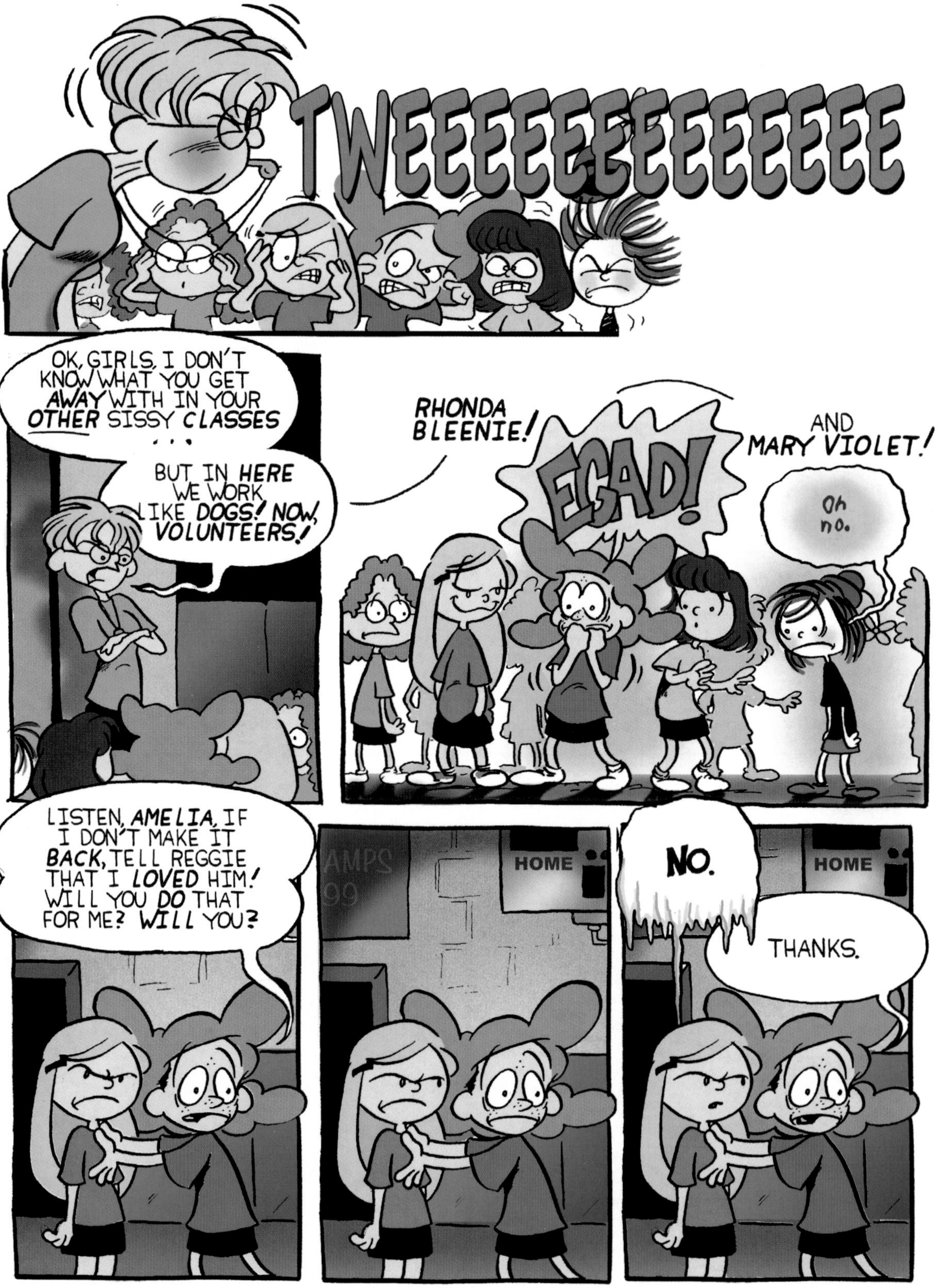
TWEEEEEEEEEEEEEEE
OK, GIRLS, I DON'T KNOW WHAT YOU GET AWAY WITH IN YOUR OTHER SISSY CLASSES . . .
BUT IN HERE WE WORK LIKE DOGS! NOW, VOLUNTEERS!
RHONDA BLEENIE!
EGAD!
AND MARY VIOLET!
Oh no.
LISTEN, AMELIA, IF I DON'T MAKE IT BACK, TELL REGGIE THAT I LOVED HIM! WILL YOU DO THAT FOR ME? WILL YOU?
HOME
NO.
HOME
THANKS.

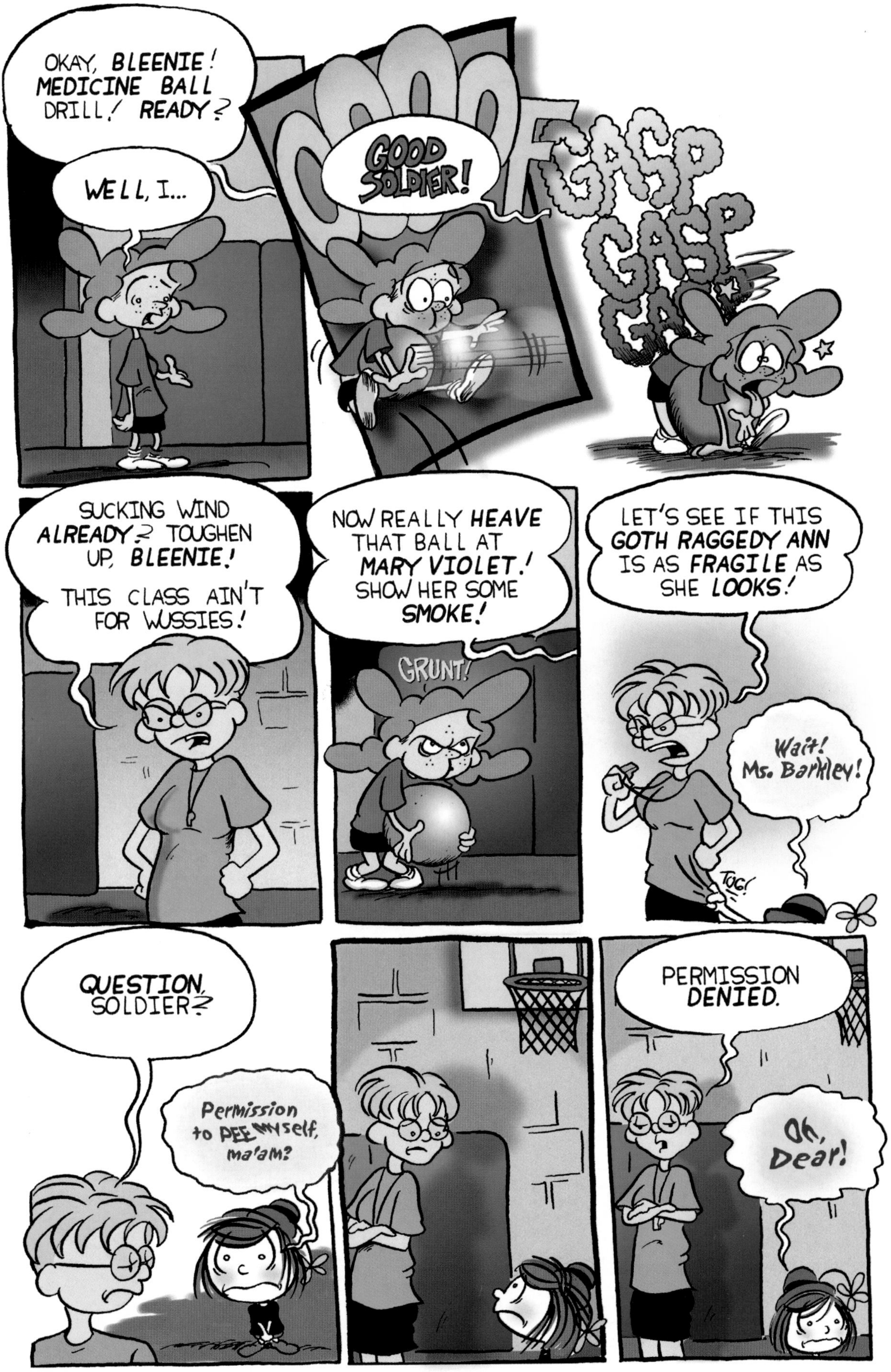
OKAY, BLEENIE! MEDICINE BALL DRILL! READY?
WELL, I...
OOOOOF
GOOD SOLDIER!
GASP GASP GASP
SUCKING WIND ALREADY? TOUGHEN UP, BLEENIE!
THIS CLASS AIN'T FOR WUSSIES!
NOW REALLY HEAVE THAT BALL AT MARY VIOLET! SHOW HER SOME SMOKE!
GRUNT!
LET'S SEE IF THIS GOTH RAGGEDY ANN IS AS FRAGILE AS SHE LOOKS!
Wait! Ms. Barkley!
TUG!
QUESTION, SOLDIER?
Permission to PEE myself, ma'am?
PERMISSION DENIED.
Oh, Dear!

This isn't good.

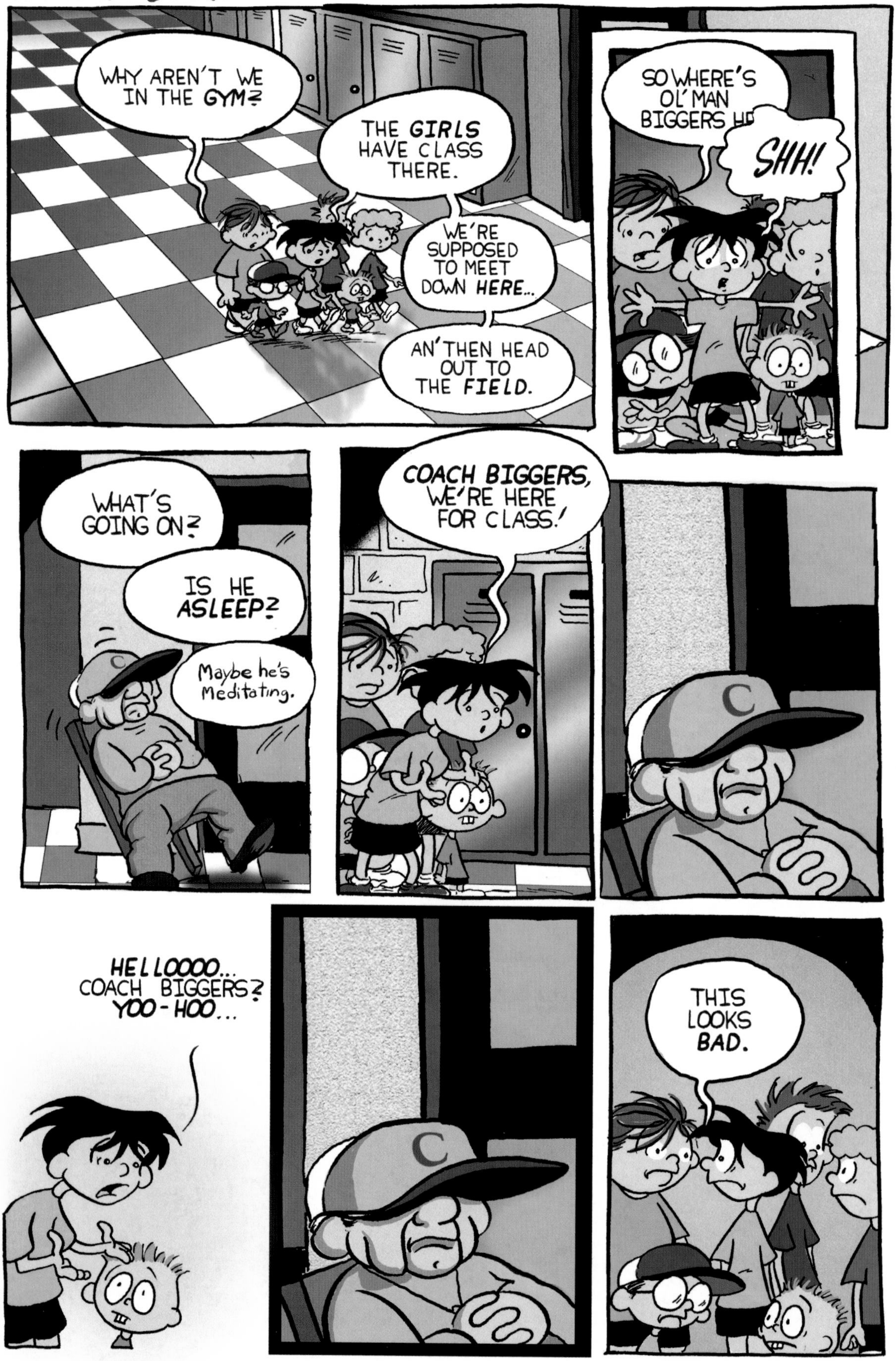
WHY AREN'T WE IN THE GYM?
THE GIRLS HAVE CLASS THERE.
WE'RE SUPPOSED TO MEET DOWN HERE...
AN' THEN HEAD OUT TO THE FIELD.
SO WHERE'S OL' MAN BIGGERS H
SHH!
WHAT'S GOING ON?
IS HE ASLEEP?
Maybe he's Meditating.
COACH BIGGERS, WE'RE HERE FOR CLASS!
HELLOOOO... COACH BIGGERS? YOO-HOO...
THIS LOOKS BAD.

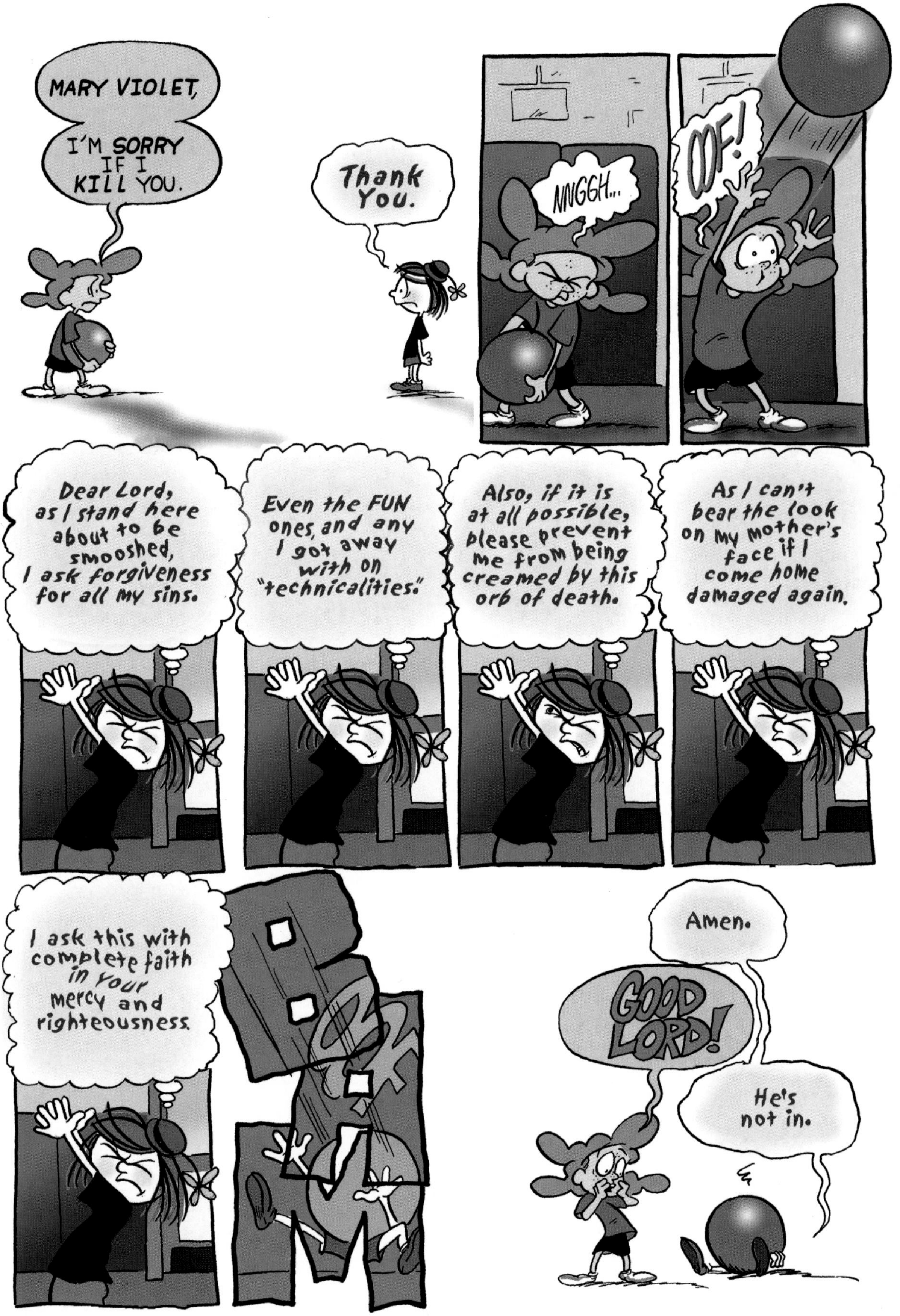
MARY VIOLET,
I'M SORRY IF I KILL YOU.
Thank You.
NNGGH...
OOF!
Dear Lord, as I stand here about to be smooshed, I ask forgiveness for all my sins.
Even the FUN ones, and any I got away with on "technicalities."
Also, if it is at all possible, please prevent me from being creamed by this orb of death.
As I can't bear the look on my mother's face if I come home damaged again.
I ask this with complete faith in your mercy and righteousness.
Amen.
GOOD LORD!
He's not in.

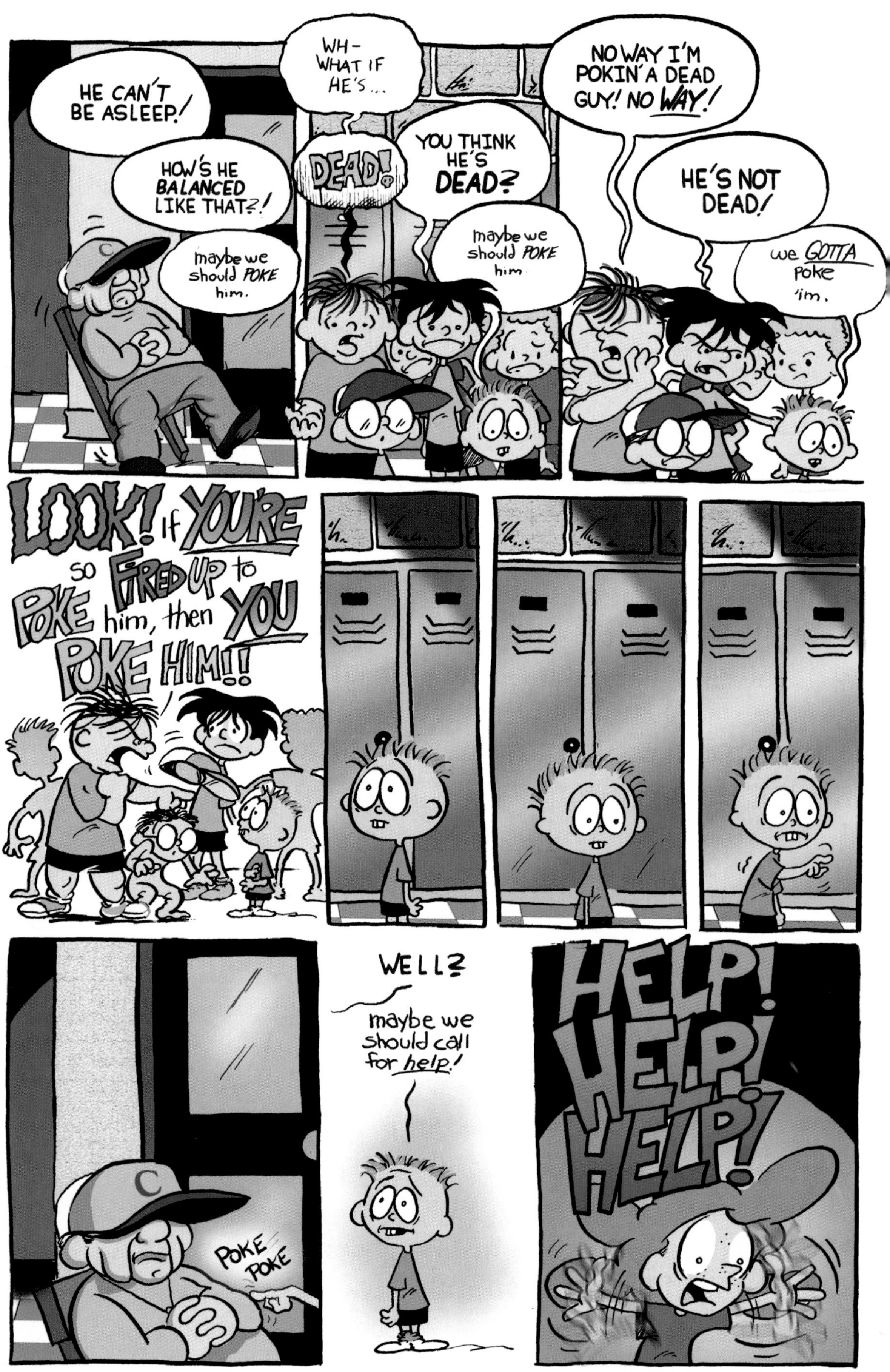
HE CAN'T BE ASLEEP!
HOW'S HE BALANCED LIKE THAT?!
maybe we should POKE him.
WH- WHAT IF HE'S...
DEAD!
YOU THINK HE'S DEAD?
maybe we should POKE him.
NO WAY I'M POKIN' A DEAD GUY! NO WAY!
HE'S NOT DEAD!
we GOTTA poke 'im.
LOOK! If YOU'RE so FIRED UP to POKE him, then YOU POKE HIM!!
POKE POKE
WELL?
maybe we should call for help!
HELP! HELP! HELP!

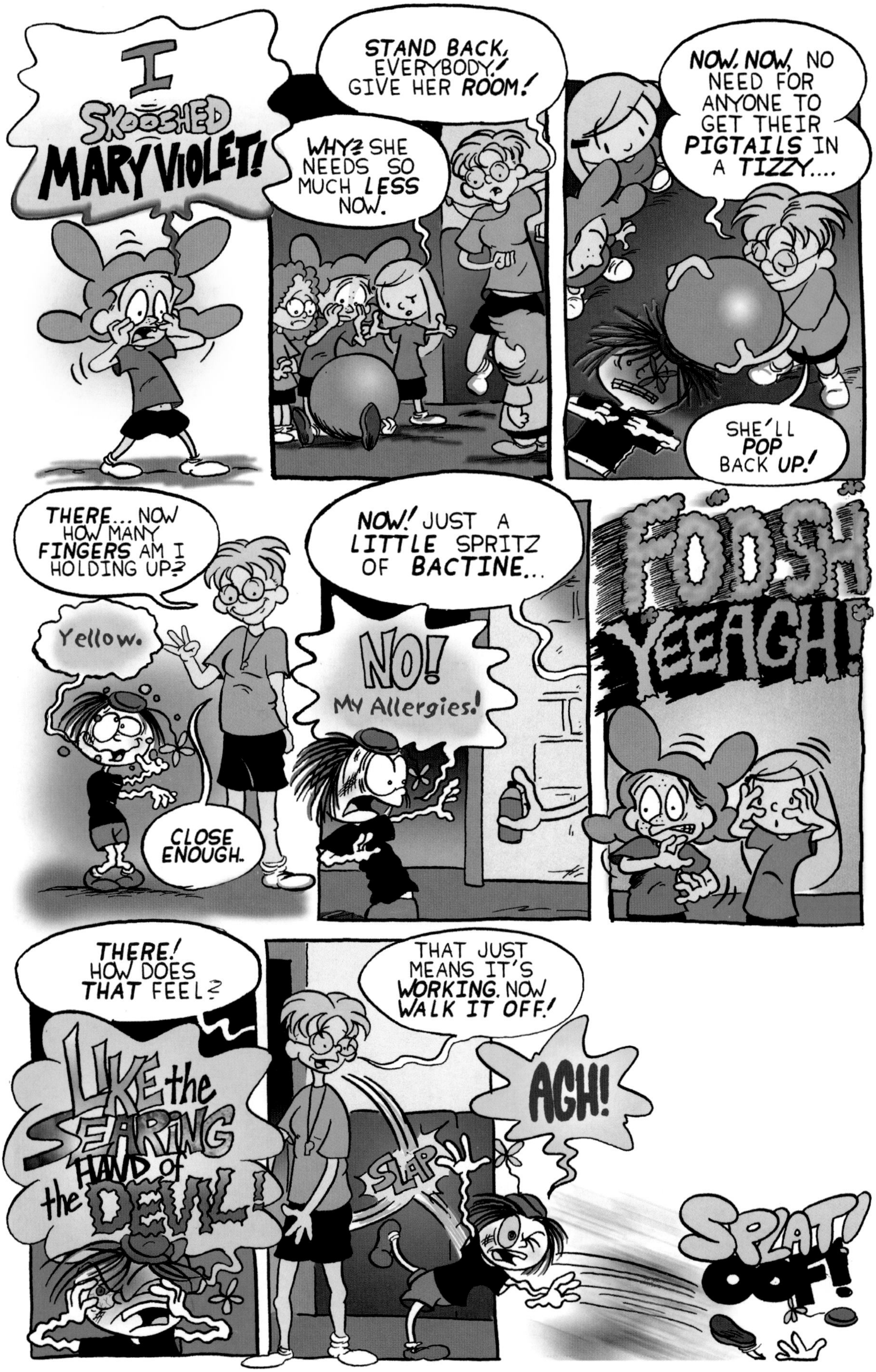
I SKOOSHED MARY VIOLET!
STAND BACK, EVERYBODY! GIVE HER ROOM!
WHY? SHE NEEDS SO MUCH LESS NOW.
NOW, NOW, NO NEED FOR ANYONE TO GET THEIR PIGTAILS IN A TIZZY....
SHE'LL POP BACK UP!
THERE... NOW HOW MANY FINGERS AM I HOLDING UP?
Yellow.
CLOSE ENOUGH.
NOW! JUST A LITTLE SPRITZ OF BACTINE...
NO! My Allergies!
FOOSH
YEEAGH!
THERE! HOW DOES THAT FEEL?
LIKE the SEARING HAND of the DEVIL!
THAT JUST MEANS IT'S WORKING. NOW WALK IT OFF!
AGH!
SLAP
SPLAT!
OOF!

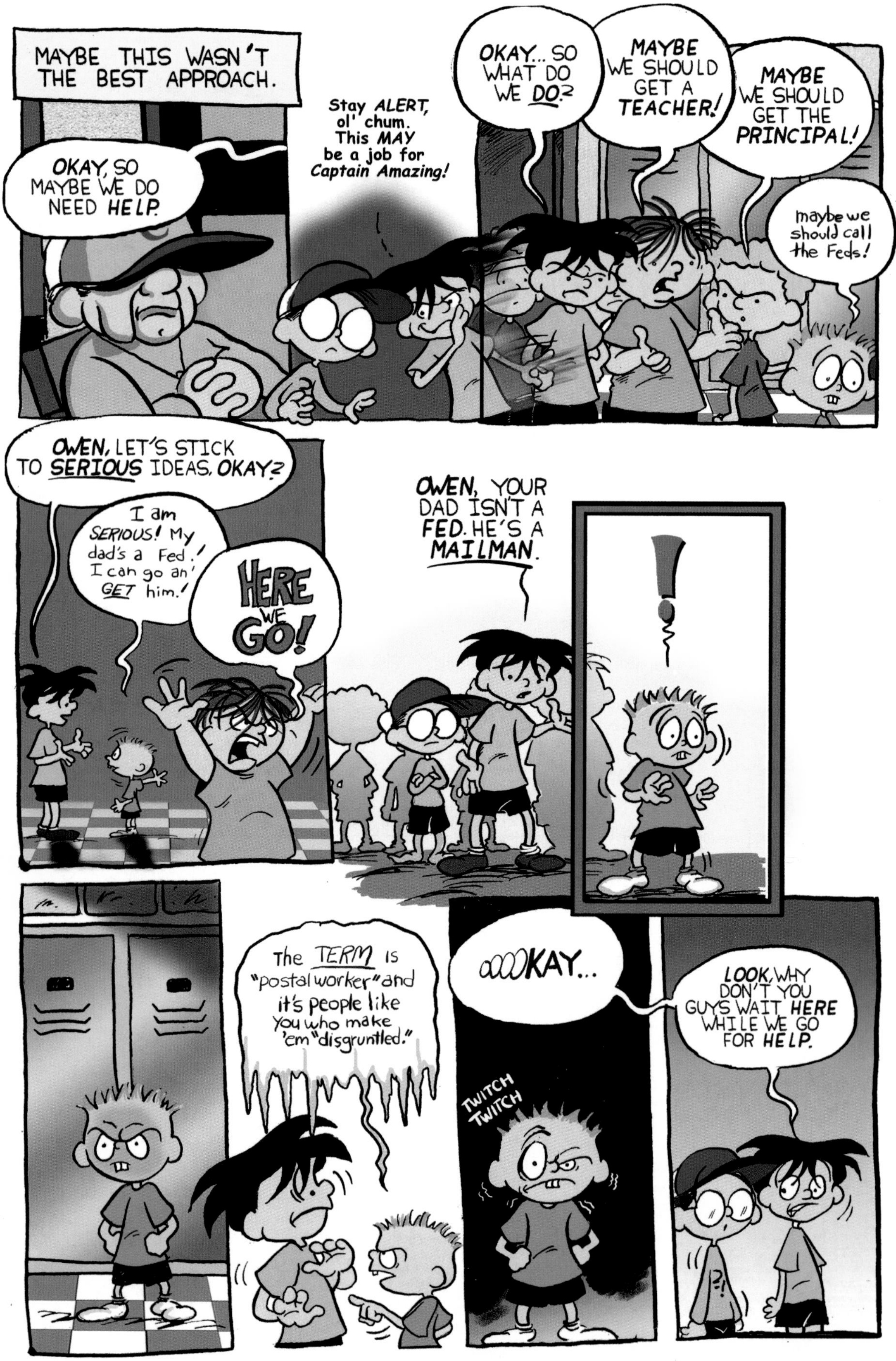
MAYBE THIS WASN'T THE BEST APPROACH.
OKAY, SO MAYBE WE DO NEED HELP.
Stay ALERT, ol' chum. This MAY be a job for Captain Amazing!
OKAY... SO WHAT DO WE DO?
MAYBE WE SHOULD GET A TEACHER!
MAYBE WE SHOULD GET THE PRINCIPAL!
maybe we should call the Feds!
OWEN, LET'S STICK TO SERIOUS IDEAS, OKAY?
I am SERIOUS! My dad's a Fed! I can go an' GET him!
HERE WE GO!
OWEN, YOUR DAD ISN'T A FED. HE'S A MAILMAN.
!
The TERM is "postal worker" and it's people like you who make 'em "disgruntled."
OOOOKAY...
TWITCH TWITCH
LOOK, WHY DON'T YOU GUYS WAIT HERE WHILE WE GO FOR HELP.
?!

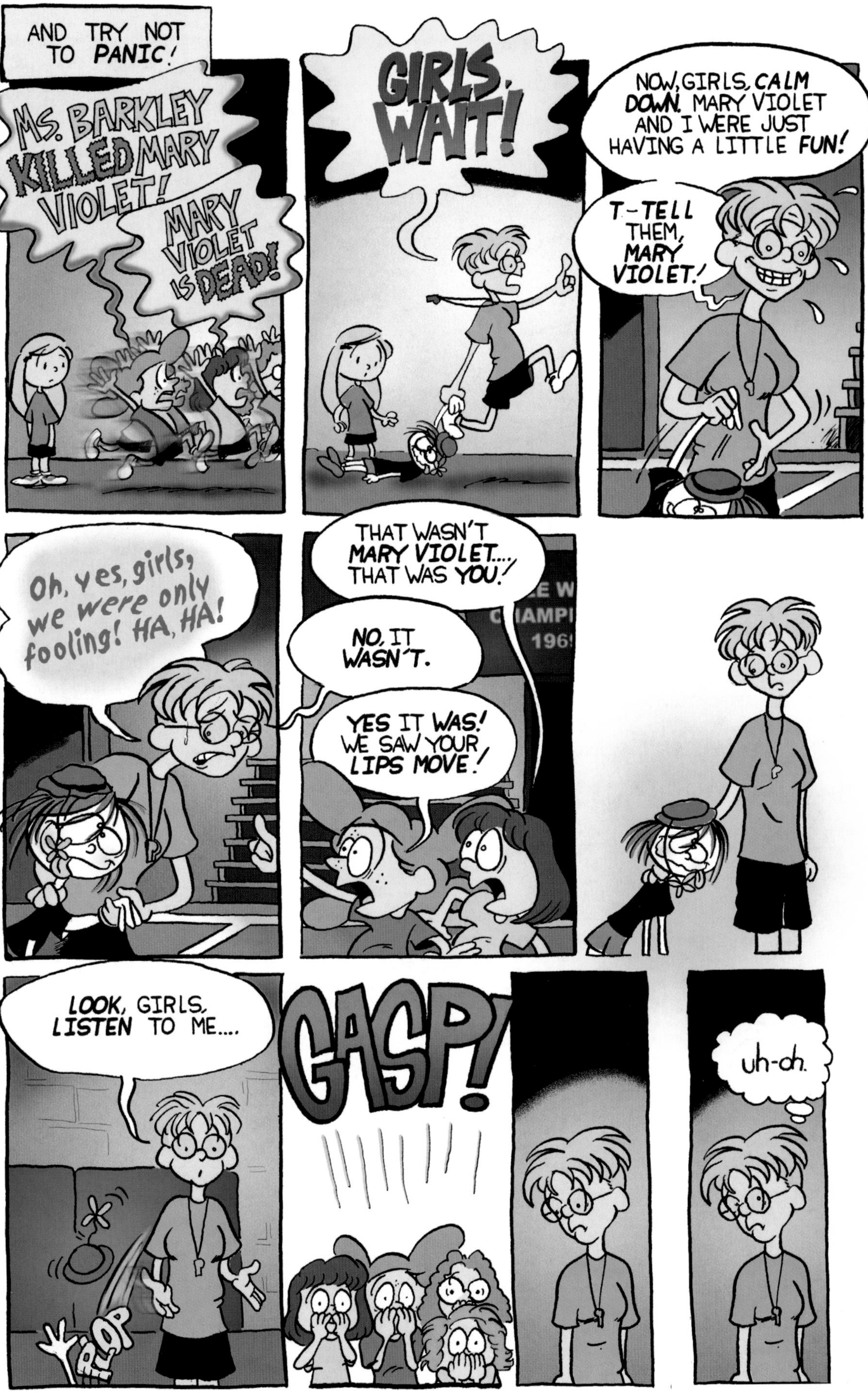
AND TRY NOT TO PANIC!
MS. BARKLEY KILLED MARY VIOLET!
MARY VIOLET IS DEAD!
GIRLS, WAIT!
NOW, GIRLS, CALM DOWN. MARY VIOLET AND I WERE JUST HAVING A LITTLE FUN!
T-TELL THEM, MARY VIOLET!
Oh, yes, girls, we were only fooling! HA, HA!
THAT WASN'T MARY VIOLET.... THAT WAS YOU!
NO, IT WASN'T.
YES IT WAS! WE SAW YOUR LIPS MOVE!
LOOK, GIRLS, LISTEN TO ME....
PLOP
GASP!
uh-oh.

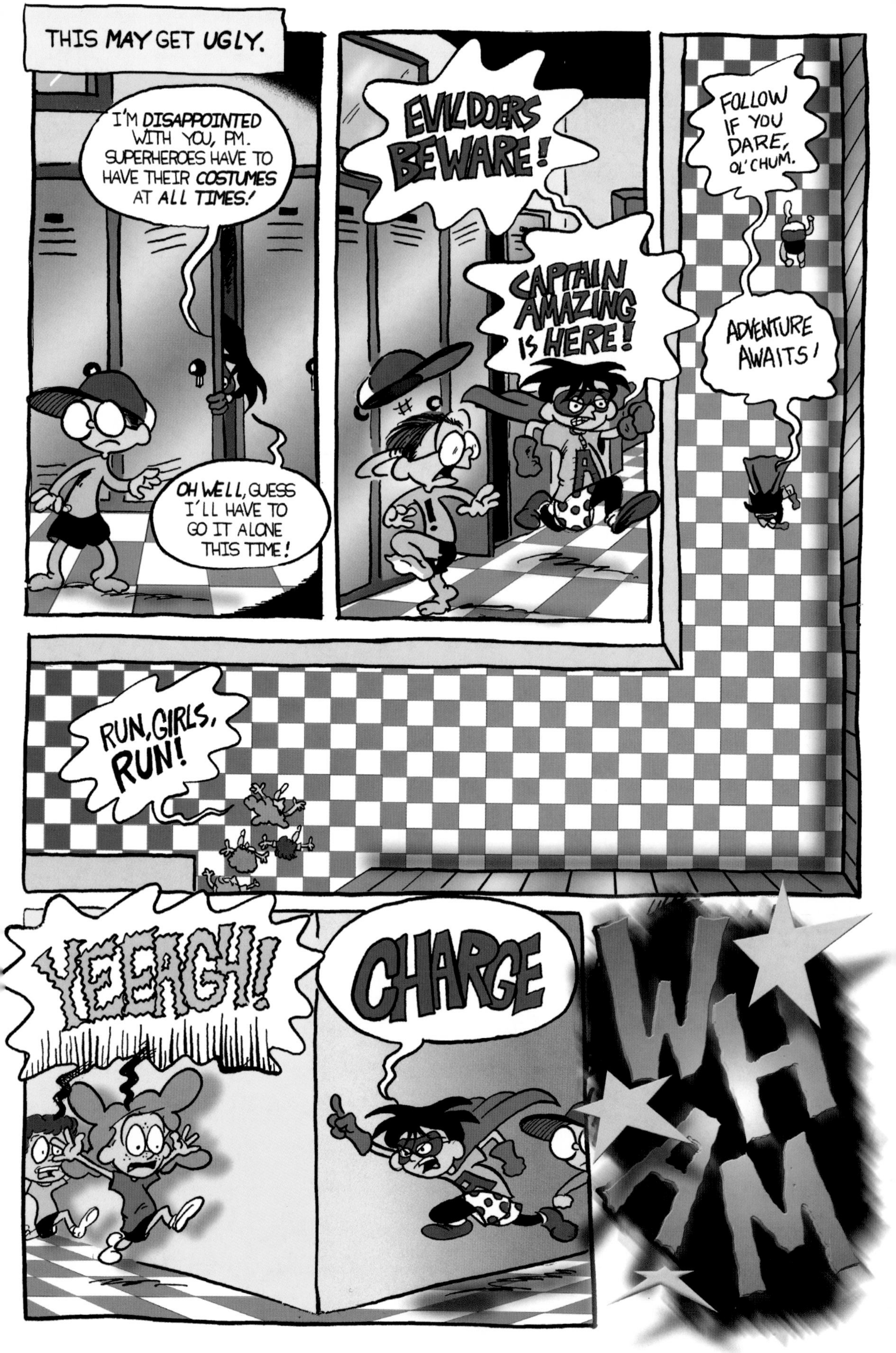
THIS MAY GET UGLY.
I'M DISAPPOINTED WITH YOU, PM. SUPERHEROES HAVE TO HAVE THEIR COSTUMES AT ALL TIMES!
OH WELL, GUESS I'LL HAVE TO GO IT ALONE THIS TIME!
EVILDOERS BEWARE!
CAPTAIN AMAZING IS HERE!
FOLLOW IF YOU DARE, OL' CHUM.
ADVENTURE AWAITS!
RUN, GIRLS, RUN!
YEEAGH!!
CHARGE
WHAM

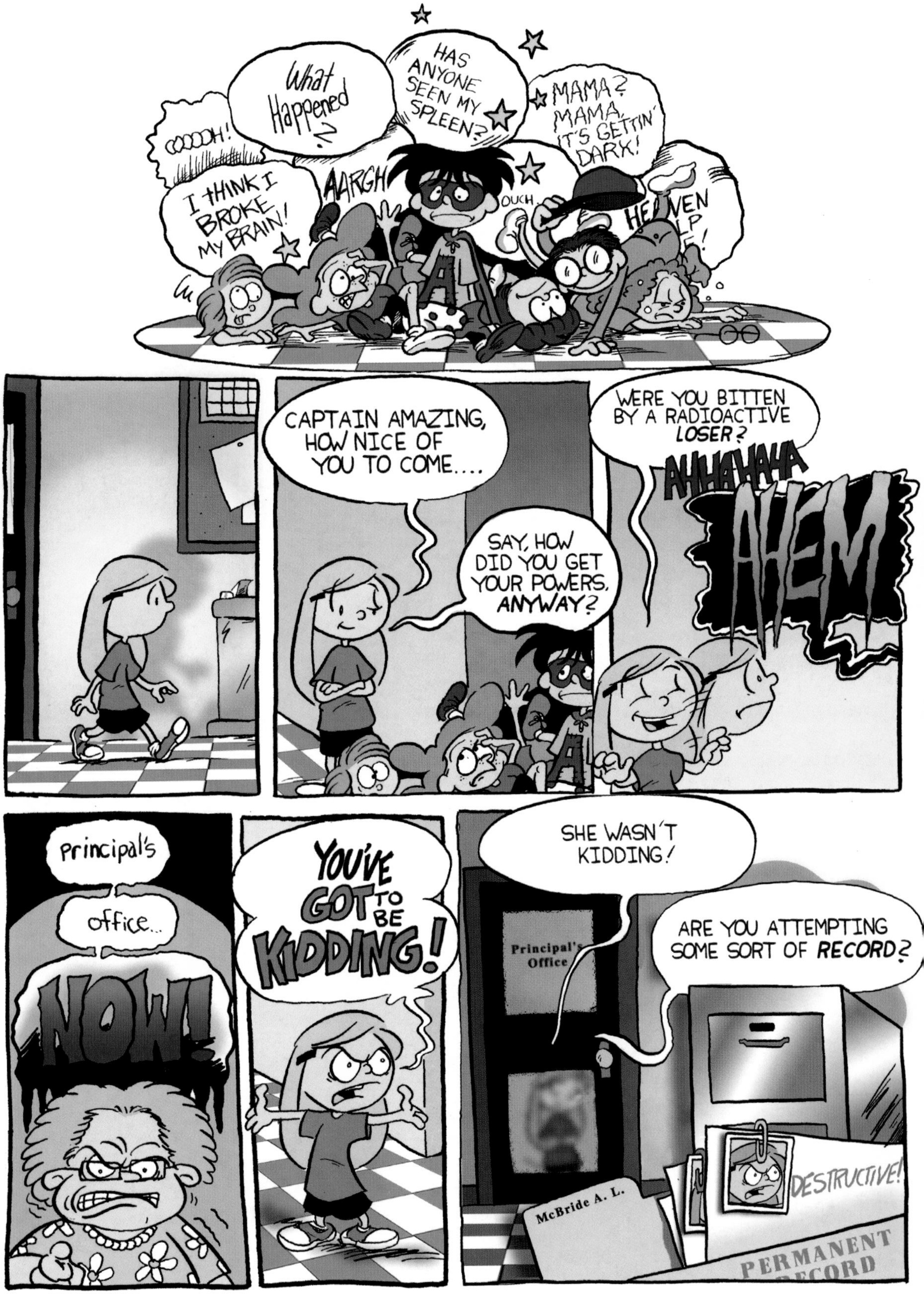

OOOOOH!
What Happened?
HAS ANYONE SEEN MY SPLEEN?
MAMA? MAMA, IT'S GETTIN' DARK!
I THINK I BROKE MY BRAIN!
AARGH
OUCH
CAPTAIN AMAZING, HOW NICE OF YOU TO COME....
SAY, HOW DID YOU GET YOUR POWERS, ANYWAY?
WERE YOU BITTEN BY A RADIOACTIVE LOSER?
AHHAHAHA
AHEM
Principal's
office...
NOW!
YOU'VE GOT TO BE KIDDING!
SHE WASN'T KIDDING!
ARE YOU ATTEMPTING SOME SORT OF RECORD?
Principal's Office
McBride A. L.
DESTRUCTIVE!
PERMANENT

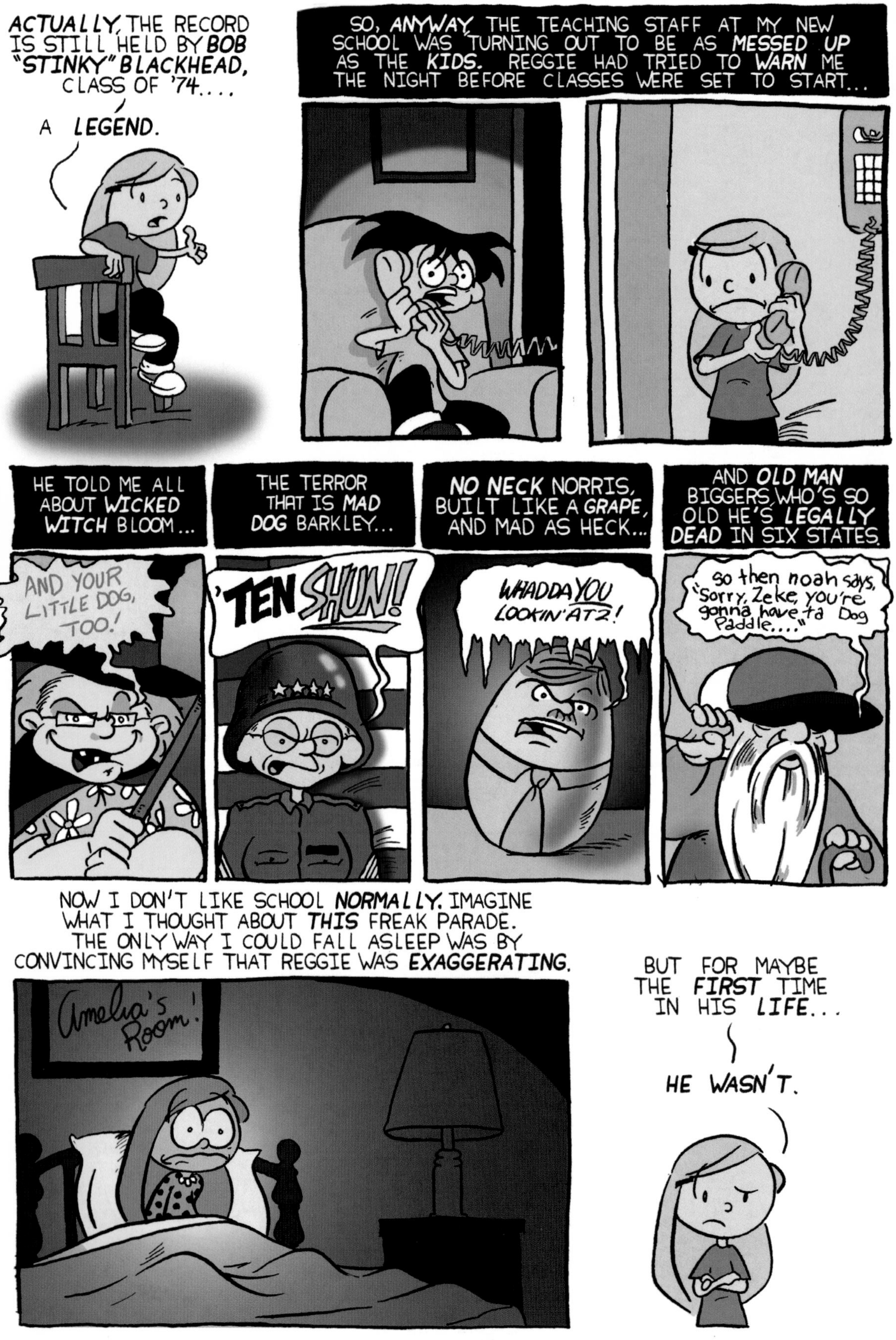
ACTUALLY, THE RECORD IS STILL HELD BY BOB "STINKY" BLACKHEAD, CLASS OF '74....
A LEGEND.
SO, ANYWAY, THE TEACHING STAFF AT MY NEW SCHOOL WAS TURNING OUT TO BE AS MESSED UP AS THE KIDS. REGGIE HAD TRIED TO WARN ME THE NIGHT BEFORE CLASSES WERE SET TO START...
HE TOLD ME ALL ABOUT WICKED WITCH BLOOM...
AND YOUR LITTLE DOG, TOO!
THE TERROR THAT IS MAD DOG BARKLEY...
'TEN SHUN!
NO NECK NORRIS, BUILT LIKE A GRAPE, AND MAD AS HECK...
WHADDA YOU LOOKIN' AT?!
AND OLD MAN BIGGERS, WHO'S SO OLD HE'S LEGALLY DEAD IN SIX STATES.
so then noah says, "Sorry, Zeke, you're gonna have ta Dog Paddle...."
NOW I DON'T LIKE SCHOOL NORMALLY. IMAGINE WHAT I THOUGHT ABOUT THIS FREAK PARADE. THE ONLY WAY I COULD FALL ASLEEP WAS BY CONVINCING MYSELF THAT REGGIE WAS EXAGGERATING.
Amelia's Room!
BUT FOR MAYBE THE FIRST TIME IN HIS LIFE...
HE WASN'T.

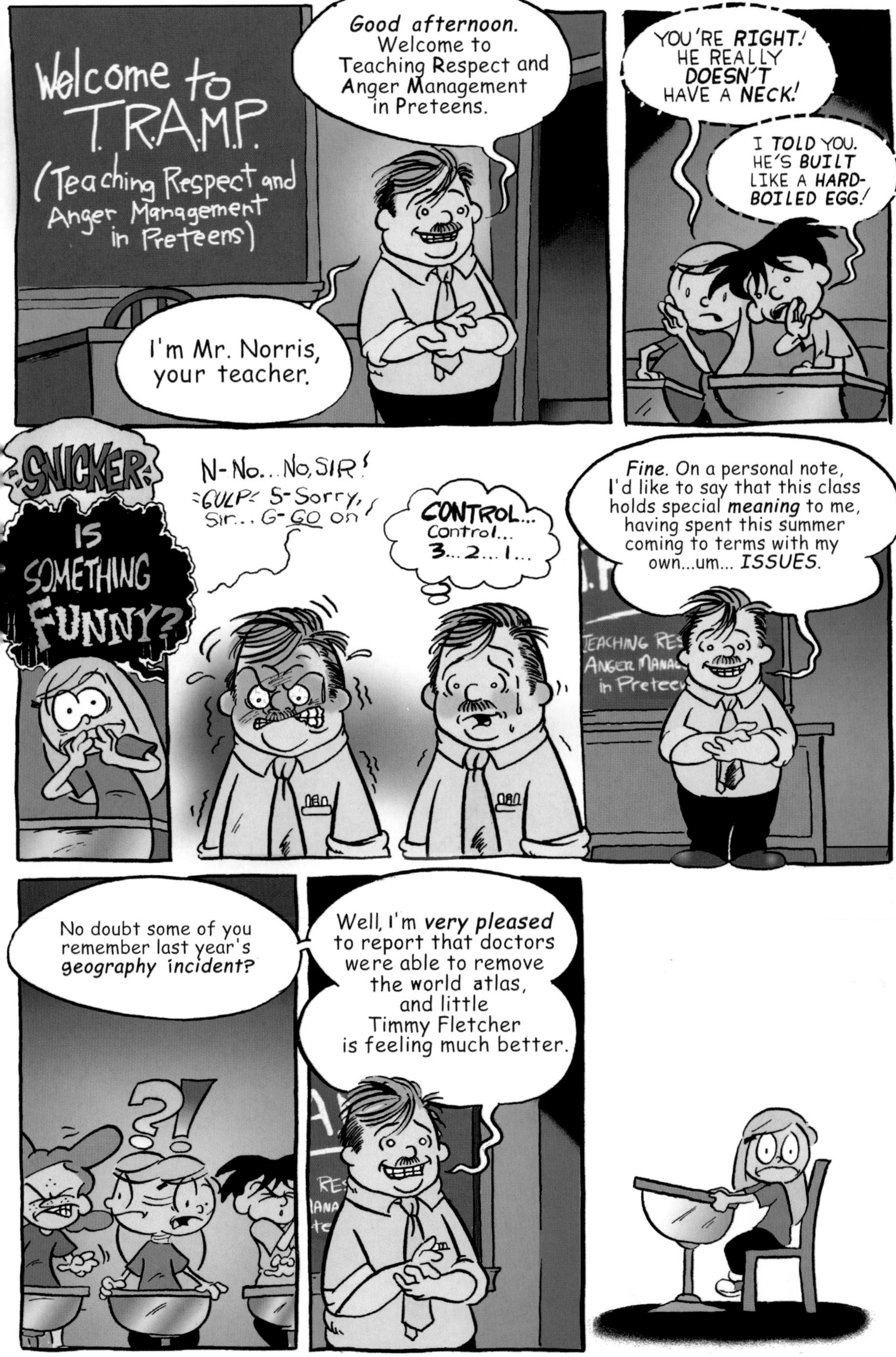
Welcome to T.R.A.M.P. (Teaching Respect and Anger Management in Preteens)
Good afternoon. Welcome to Teaching Respect and Anger Management in Preteens.
I'm Mr. Norris, your teacher.
YOU'RE RIGHT! HE REALLY DOESN'T HAVE A NECK!
I TOLD YOU. HE'S BUILT LIKE A HARD-BOILED EGG!
SNICKER
IS SOMETHING FUNNY?
N-No... No, SIR! GULP S-Sorry, Sir... G-GO on
CONTROL... Control... 3... 2... 1...
Fine. On a personal note, I'd like to say that this class holds special meaning to me, having spent this summer coming to terms with my own...um... ISSUES.
No doubt some of you remember last year's geography incident?
?!
Well, I'm very pleased to report that doctors were able to remove the world atlas, and little Timmy Fletcher is feeling much better.

Well, anyway, let's just put all of that *behind* us.

Umm... no *pun* intended.

To get started, I thought we'd take a little *"personality test"* to get the feel of the group.

Show of hands... If caught in a disagreement with another, how many of you would...

A. Seek resolution by expressing your opinion verbally yet forcefully.

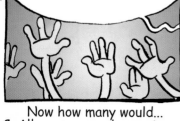

Hmm...interesting... interesting...

B. Keep silent and attempt to avoid any conflict whatsoever.

Yes, yes... fascinating.

Simply fascinating.

Now how many would... C. Allow anger and resentment to fester and build, eventually swearing a lifelong vendetta against the other person and all others like them.

Aa Bb Cc Dd Ee Ff Gg Hh

Very good, I...

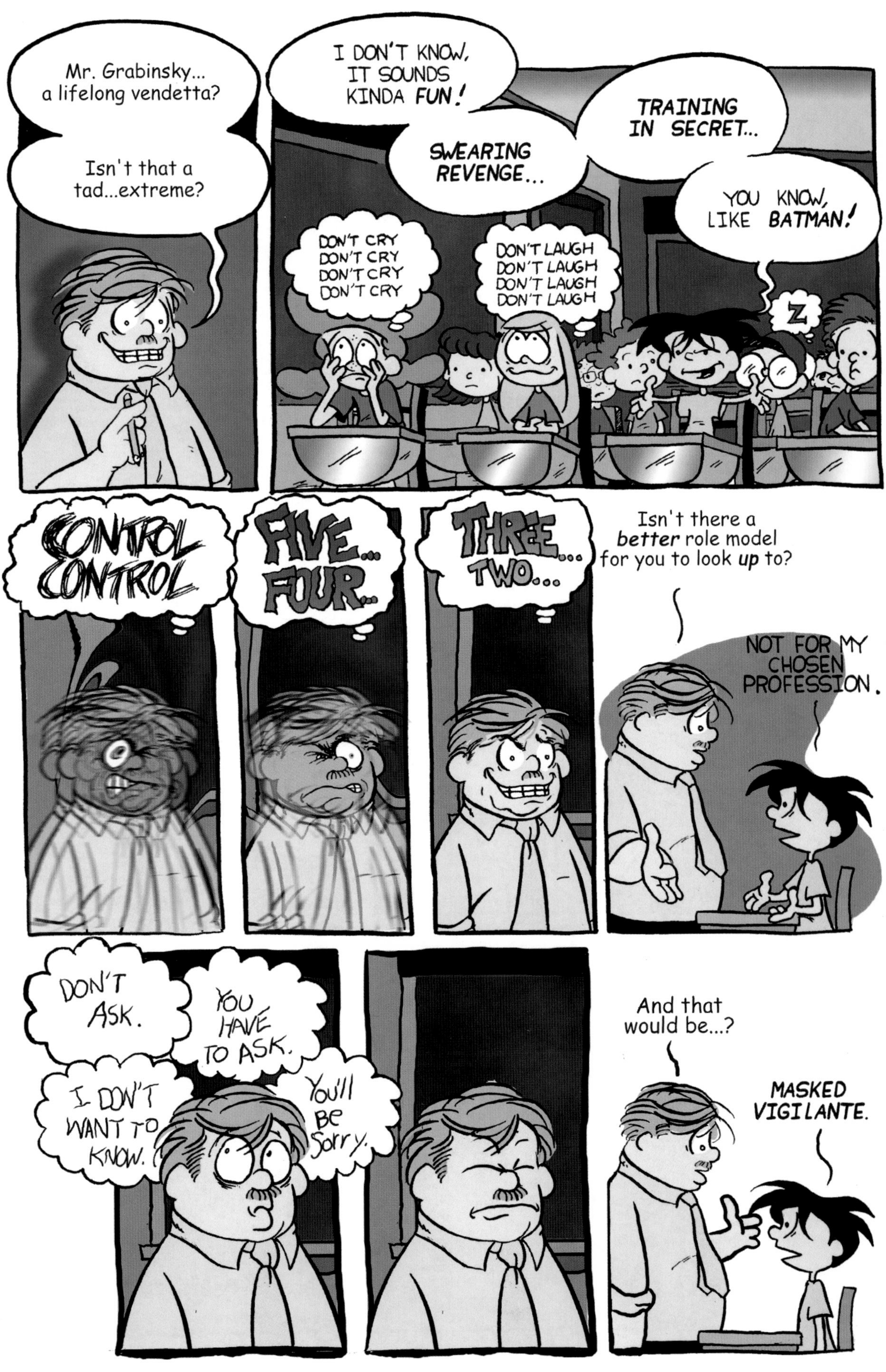

Mr. Grabinsky... a lifelong vendetta?
Isn't that a tad...extreme?
I DON'T KNOW, IT SOUNDS KINDA FUN!
SWEARING REVENGE...
TRAINING IN SECRET...
YOU KNOW, LIKE BATMAN!
DON'T CRY DON'T CRY DON'T CRY DON'T CRY
DON'T LAUGH DON'T LAUGH DON'T LAUGH DON'T LAUGH
Z
CONTROL CONTROL
FIVE... FOUR...
THREE... TWO...
Isn't there a better role model for you to look up to?
NOT FOR MY CHOSEN PROFESSION.
DON'T ASK.
YOU HAVE TO ASK.
I DON'T WANT TO KNOW.
You'll Be Sorry.
And that would be...?
MASKED VIGILANTE.

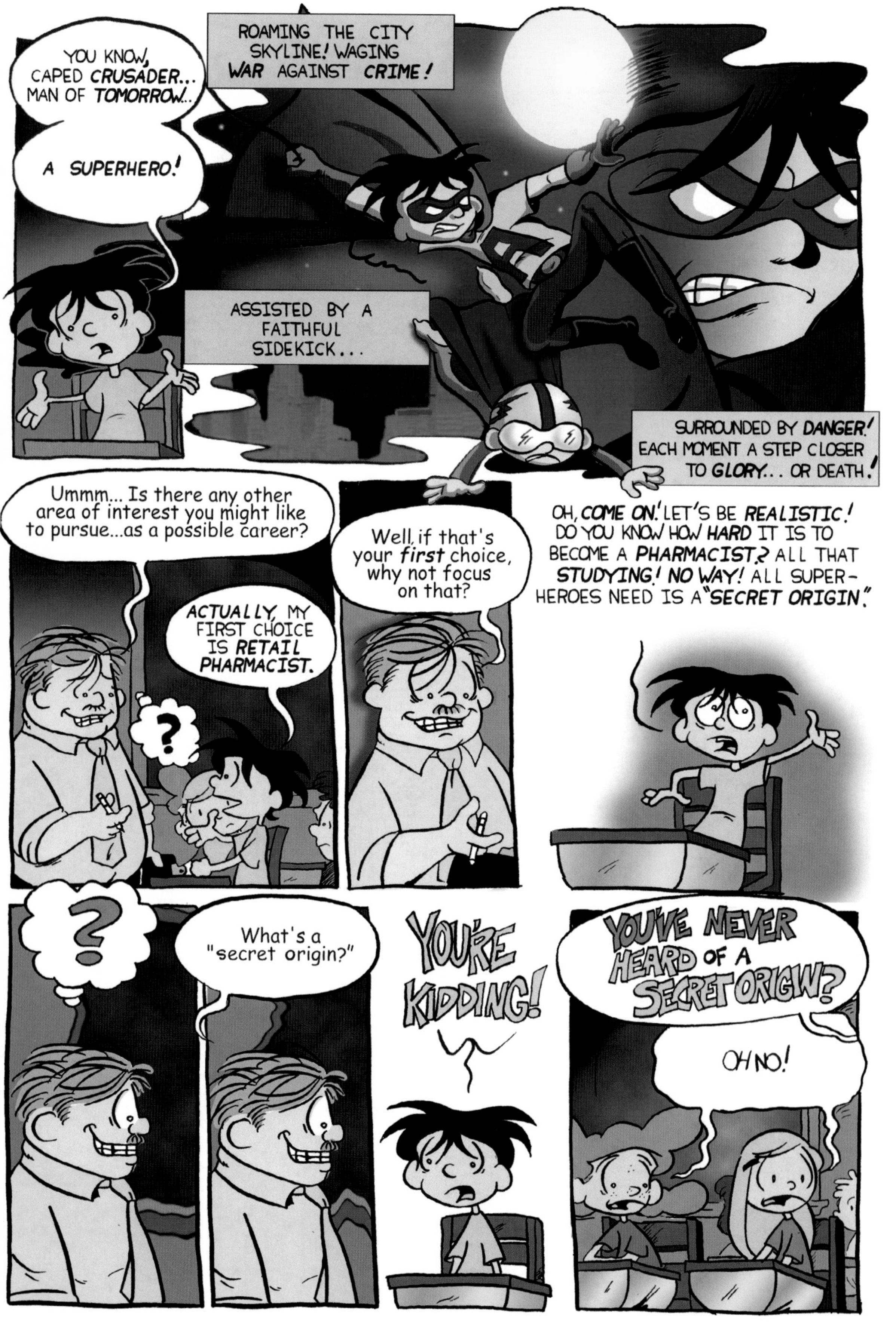
YOU KNOW, CAPED CRUSADER... MAN OF TOMORROW...
ROAMING THE CITY SKYLINE! WAGING WAR AGAINST CRIME!
A SUPERHERO!
ASSISTED BY A FAITHFUL SIDEKICK...
SURROUNDED BY DANGER! EACH MOMENT A STEP CLOSER TO GLORY... OR DEATH!
Ummm... Is there any other area of interest you might like to pursue...as a possible career?
?
ACTUALLY, MY FIRST CHOICE IS RETAIL PHARMACIST.
Well, if that's your first choice, why not focus on that?
OH, COME ON! LET'S BE REALISTIC! DO YOU KNOW HOW HARD IT IS TO BECOME A PHARMACIST? ALL THAT STUDYING! NO WAY! ALL SUPER-HEROES NEED IS A "SECRET ORIGIN."
?
What's a "secret origin?"
YOU'RE KIDDING!
YOU'VE NEVER HEARD OF A SECRET ORIGIN?
OH NO!

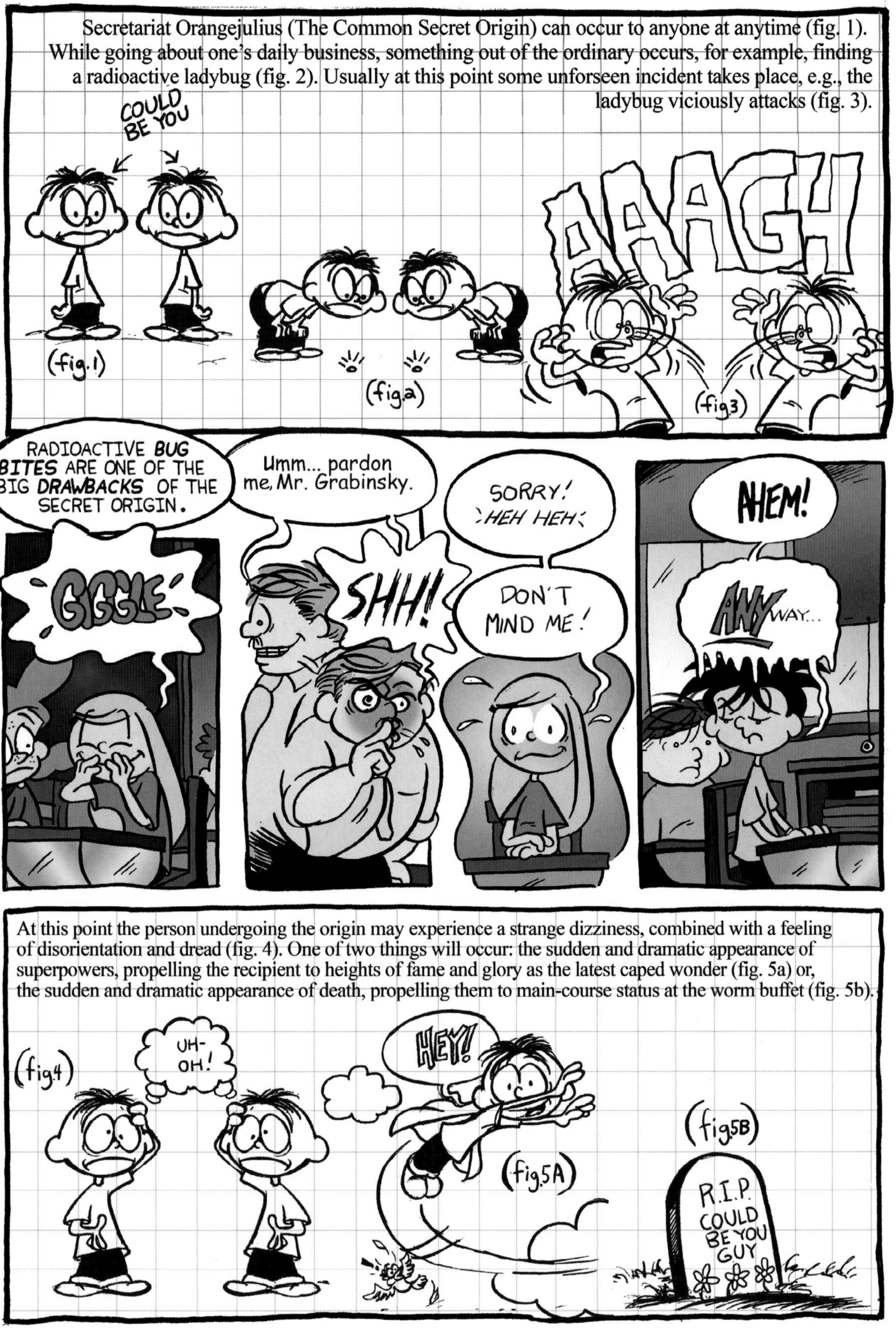
Secretariat Orangejulius (The Common Secret Origin) can occur to anyone at anytime (fig. 1). While going about one's daily business, something out of the ordinary occurs, for example, finding a radioactive ladybug (fig. 2). Usually at this point some unforseen incident takes place, e.g., the ladybug viciously attacks (fig. 3).
COULD BE YOU
(fig.1)
(fig.2)
AAGH
(fig.3)
RADIOACTIVE BUG BITES ARE ONE OF THE BIG DRAWBACKS OF THE SECRET ORIGIN.
GIGGLE
Umm... pardon me, Mr. Grabinsky.
SHH!
SORRY! HEH HEH
DON'T MIND ME!
AHEM!
ANYWAY...
At this point the person undergoing the origin may experience a strange dizziness, combined with a feeling of disorientation and dread (fig. 4). One of two things will occur: the sudden and dramatic appearance of superpowers, propelling the recipient to heights of fame and glory as the latest caped wonder (fig. 5a) or, the sudden and dramatic appearance of death, propelling them to main-course status at the worm buffet (fig. 5b).
(fig.4)
UH-OH!
HEY!
(fig.5A)
(fig.5B)
R.I.P. COULD BE YOU GUY

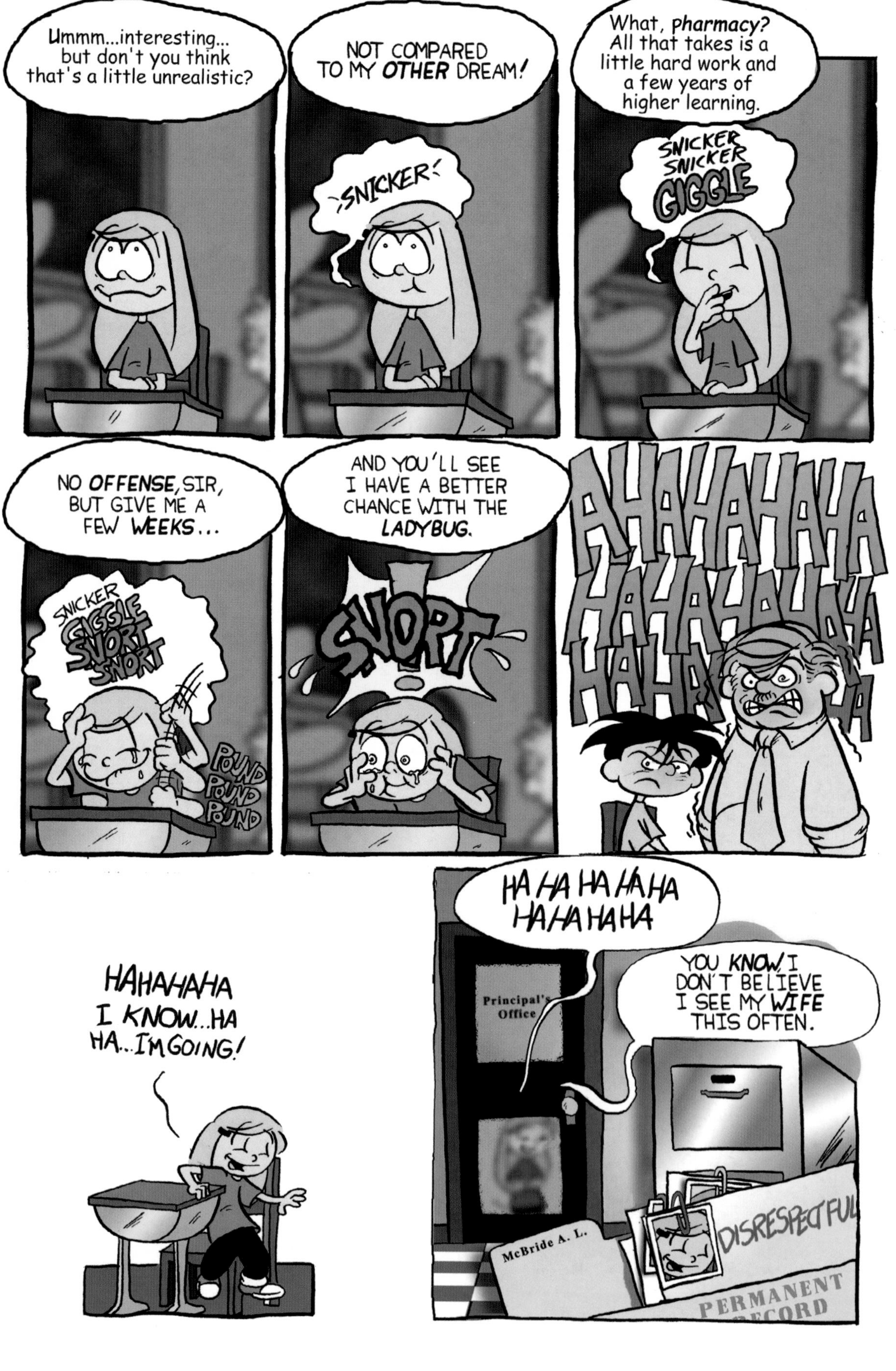
Ummm...interesting... but don't you think that's a little unrealistic?
NOT COMPARED TO MY OTHER DREAM!
SNICKER!
What, pharmacy? All that takes is a little hard work and a few years of higher learning.
SNICKER SNICKER GIGGLE
NO OFFENSE, SIR, BUT GIVE ME A FEW WEEKS...
SNICKER GIGGLE SNORT SNORT
POUND POUND POUND
AND YOU'LL SEE I HAVE A BETTER CHANCE WITH THE LADYBUG.
SNORT
AHAHAHAHA HAHAHAHAHA HAHA
HAHAHAHA I KNOW...HA HA...I'M GOING!
HA HA HA HA HA HA HA HA HA
YOU KNOW, I DON'T BELIEVE I SEE MY WIFE THIS OFTEN.
Principal's Office
McBride A. L.
DISRESPECTFUL
PERMANENT RECORD

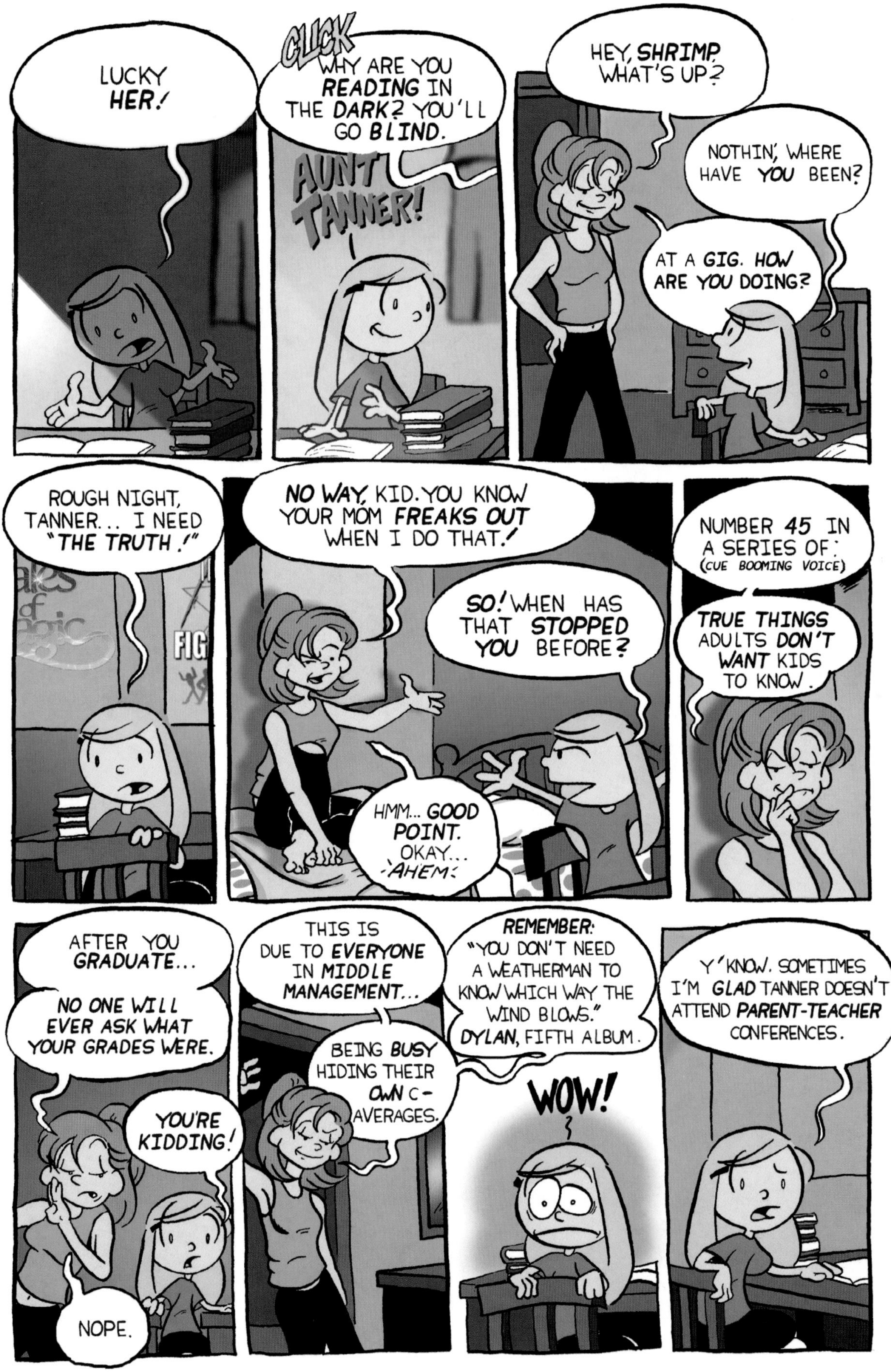
LUCKY HER!
CLICK
WHY ARE YOU READING IN THE DARK? YOU'LL GO BLIND.
AUNT TANNER!
HEY, SHRIMP, WHAT'S UP?
NOTHIN', WHERE HAVE YOU BEEN?
AT A GIG. HOW ARE YOU DOING?
ROUGH NIGHT, TANNER... I NEED "THE TRUTH!"
NO WAY, KID. YOU KNOW YOUR MOM FREAKS OUT WHEN I DO THAT!
SO! WHEN HAS THAT STOPPED YOU BEFORE?
HMM... GOOD POINT. OKAY... AHEM
NUMBER 45 IN A SERIES OF: (CUE BOOMING VOICE)
TRUE THINGS ADULTS DON'T WANT KIDS TO KNOW.
AFTER YOU GRADUATE...
NO ONE WILL EVER ASK WHAT YOUR GRADES WERE.
YOU'RE KIDDING!
NOPE.
THIS IS DUE TO EVERYONE IN MIDDLE MANAGEMENT...
BEING BUSY HIDING THEIR OWN C-AVERAGES.
REMEMBER: "YOU DON'T NEED A WEATHERMAN TO KNOW WHICH WAY THE WIND BLOWS." DYLAN, FIFTH ALBUM.
WOW!
Y'KNOW, SOMETIMES I'M GLAD TANNER DOESN'T ATTEND PARENT-TEACHER CONFERENCES.

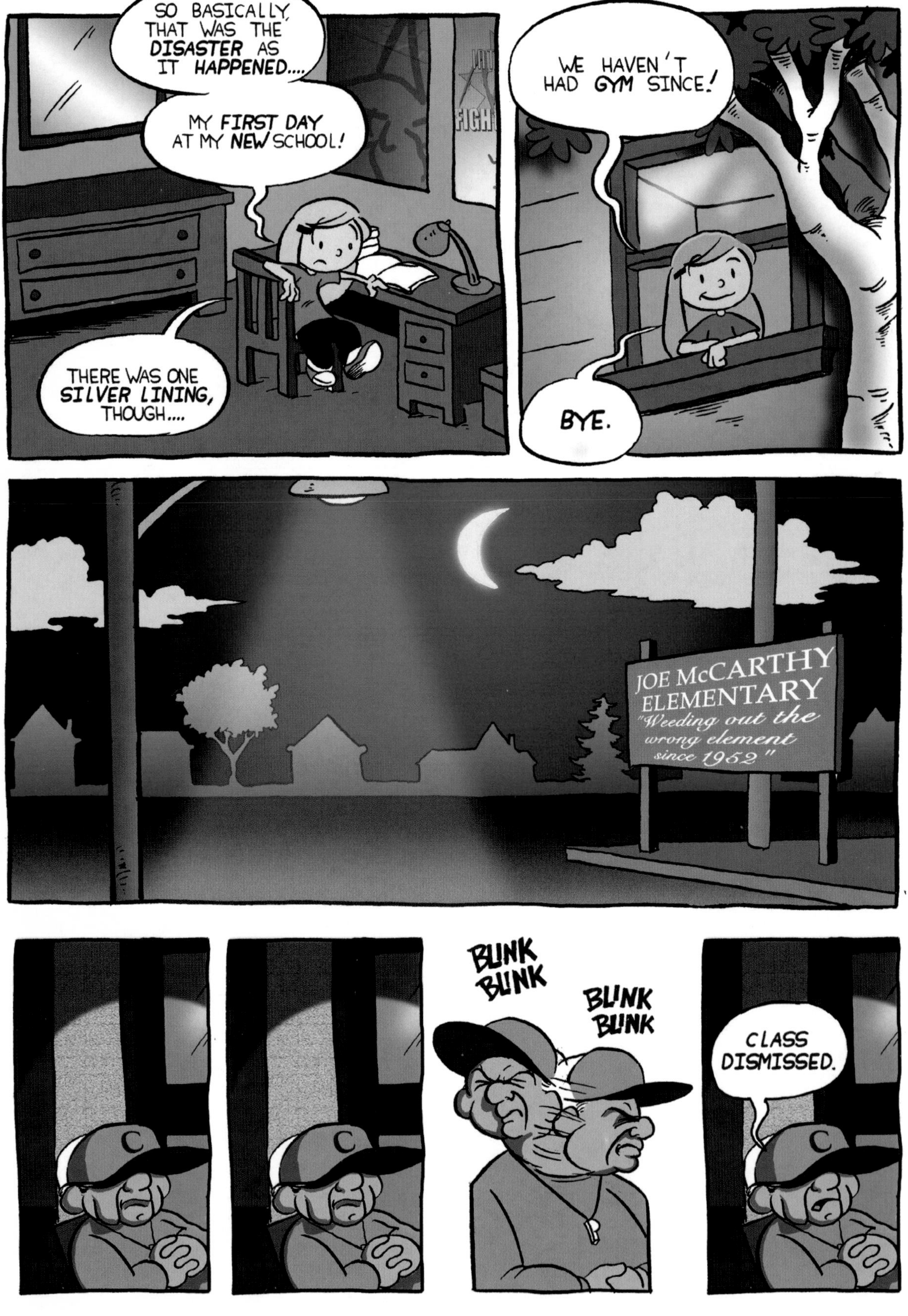
SO BASICALLY, THAT WAS THE DISASTER AS IT HAPPENED....
MY FIRST DAY AT MY NEW SCHOOL!
THERE WAS ONE SILVER LINING, THOUGH....
WE HAVEN'T HAD GYM SINCE!
BYE.
JOE McCARTHY ELEMENTARY "Weeding out the wrong element since 1952"
BLINK BLINK
BLINK BLINK
CLASS DISMISSED.